Pride Publishing books by Matthew J. Metzger

Single Books
Best Behaviour
Enough

I0542702

Starting Over
The Divorce
The Other Man
The Wedding
The Third Date

Starting Over

THE THIRD DATE

MATTHEW J. METZGER

The Third Date
ISBN # 978-1-83943-875-2
©Copyright Matthew J. Metzger 2020
Cover Art by Erin Dameron-Hill ©Copyright March 2020
Interior text design by Claire Siemaszkiewicz
Pride Publishing

THE
THIRD DATE

Dedication

For Rebecca, with my eternal thanks for all your patience!

Prologue

It was raining.

Gabriel sulked by the door, scowling at the deluge. It wasn't just raining. It was *pissing* it down. The force of the downpour was so strong that a haze lingered two inches above the tarmac.

Me: Pleeeeeaase tell me you're done with that meeting now???

No reply. Great. He sighed. Nothing else for it. Aled was at work for another three hours, and Kevin was working out in Bradford all week. Sighing, he rummaged for his keys and pulled up the collar of his coat.

The bike rack was at least in a shelter, albeit that rainwater was running across the floor in rivers. His Converse were soaked through in seconds, and he grumbled as he wrestled with the padlock. On days like today, he figured Aled had a point about the merits of a car over a mountain bike.

But *only* days like today.

His phone buzzed as he put his helmet on, and he paused in the relative dryness of the shelter to slide it out of his pocket, hoping it would be Kevin back from Bradford early, or Aled promising to come and pick him up in half an hour.

Instead, he smiled goofily.

Chris: Can you get the first week in July off? I don't want to wait until November to spend some real time with you x

His heart picked up a little bit at the kiss. He'd known Chris almost two years, but there was just something sweet about him that got under Gabriel's skin. Aled was the hot coals of a fire, alluring and intense but dangerous, too. Chris was more like the steady burning of a candle — quiet and understated, but luxuriously warm if one knew how to shelter the flame.

And Gabriel had both of them, all to himself.

Me: I can try :) You're always welcome to spend your days off up here, though, even if I'm working x

Chris: Might be a bit awkward, just me and Aled in a room while you're at work!

"Honestly," Gabriel muttered. "Two years, you want to get over yourself yet?"

Me: He only bites if you ask very, very nicely ;)

Two years, and Chris had still probably only been in Aled's company for a collective two hours.

Chris: I'm good, thanks x

Gabriel rolled his eyes and tucked his phone back into the inside pocket of his jacket, where it stood a fighting chance of not drowning in the deluge. At least there was a hot shower waiting when he got home. And Aled was stuck in a meeting from one until five with the entire board, which meant he'd be in a savage mood when he got home. The sex was going to be fan*tastic*.

That, more than anything, got Gabriel up on the bike. Kickstand up, he rolled out of the shelter and was instantly hit with an icy-cold deluge. He grimaced. It was gloomy enough that the lights flickered into life as he wrestled the bike over the bank and down onto the side road. He opted for the main road rather than his more usual back streets. It was faster — and in this grim excuse for weather, Gabriel would take all the faster that he could get.

The phone started ringing as he surged over the crest and onto the main road, and he began to coast down the slope towards the town centre. It stopped as he passed the Lupset turning, but started again as he shot through the next set of lights. Kevin must be done in Bradford, then. Aled rang once then texted. Chris never rang at all. Gabriel ignored it, frowning as the tyres skidded as he passed into the bus and bike lane. He squeezed the brakes gently, felt the wheels slow, and felt the lack of response when it came to actual speed. Great. The amount of water on the roads was affecting the tyres' grip.

"Thank fuck for a long weekend," he muttered. He wasn't back in work for four days, and he had every intention of staying in the flat for all four of them. A long soak in the bath. Closing all the blinds and parading around naked. In fact, he wasn't even going to leave the flat for Kevin. If Kevin wanted to play, then —

Something flashed out of the corner of Gabriel's eye. Lights. He slammed on the brakes and heard the squeal of rubber underneath him. Felt the bike smash sideways on slick tarmac.

A horn blared.

Something —

He blinked. There was rainwater on his face, and he could hear —

"You with me, son? Can you hear me? Can you hear me, son?"

Yes.

Sirens. There was an engine running nearby. People talking.

"Ambulance is nearly here, son. Can you hear me?"

He blinked again. The red tinge cleared a little. There was a ghostly-white face above him. A pothole was cupping one cheek, and a clammy hand the other. Across a thousand miles of bouncing water, he could see something white resting in the road.

It was half of his helmet.

Chapter One

"No," Aled said.

Immediately, the temperature in the ward dropped by about fifteen degrees. Next door's visitors stopped chattering. The nurse fidgeted awkwardly with the drip. The doctor stuck out both chest and chin in the universal display of smug arrogance.

And Gabriel looked at him like Aled was dogshit on the bottom of his shoe.

"*Yes*," said Gabriel.

Aled pinched the bridge of his nose and exhaled heavily.

He was too tired for this. Eight weeks of sitting at Gabriel's bedside had taken its toll. The sleepless nights. The lonely house. Echoes of the phone call from the hospital the day of the accident replaying in the dark like a song on loop. The fortnight trying to remember how to pray, because if it would bring Gabriel back then Aled would convert to any religion going. The tears when Gabriel had finally woken up —

and not only woken up but had looked at Aled and known who he was. What he was. Why he was there.

The rollercoaster of emotions—fear, sorrow, joy, anger, impotent grief—had gone on too long, and now he was running on empty. Aled was too tired for this. Too shattered to handle the inevitable rebellion, now that hospital-hating Gabriel had finally decided that he'd had enough.

Because of course, he'd decided far too soon.

"Be reasonable," Aled said. "You can't—"

"I am being perfectly *fucking* reasonable," Gabriel spat.

"Yeah, you sound it."

"Shut it. Either you take me home, or I'm calling Kevin and he will."

Right, Aled thought. Because Kevin was going to tell him anything different. Gabriel's arm was still in a soft support brace. His thick, dark hair was little more than a fluffy buzzcut, the savage scar glowing pink in a great arc over his left ear. A grey quality haunted his skin, and there were heavy bags under his usually beautiful eyes. The stack of kidney dishes on his table were ready and waiting for the next bout of throwing up.

He looked *ill*.

"Kevin will only tell you exactly what I'm trying to tell you."

"But he'll fucking take me home!"

The doctor excused himself. The nurse scuttled away and pulled the curtains shut. The visit was over, and Gabriel's desperate need to be discharged wasn't going to happen today. The doctor came once and only once, come hell or high water.

Aled sat back in the chair with a deep sigh, with no more allies to help back up his position, and shook his head.

"I know you don't want to be here anymore," he said. "But you can hardly walk to the bathroom without falling over. Give it a few more—"

"What, weeks? That's what it's going to take. Weeks. I can't stay here for weeks with those bitches calling me Gabby and that smug prick sneering at me every time he deigns to show his face. They think I'm scum. I *feel* like scum."

Aled winced.

Gabriel didn't like the medical establishment at the best of times, and eight weeks with a head injury after being hit by a bus wasn't anyone's definition of 'the best of times'. He'd come away from the accident lucky—for one, he hadn't been killed—but as the weeks had bled by, the mutiny had slowly swelled.

Gabriel was transgender, so his relationship with doctors was not a pretty one. He hated going to the GP, never mind the hospital. Aled was reasonably sure he'd never plumped for a hysterectomy purely because it meant talking to more doctors. And these last eight weeks had done absolutely nothing to repair said ugly relationship. The nurses all called him Gabby or Miss Lazarri. The doctor had a permanently curled lip, although Aled suspected he looked at every patient like that. He'd been put originally into a female ward, and it was only when the other women had complained about the man in the third cubicle that he'd been moved into a mixed ward. The idea of putting him in a men's ward was apparently out of the question, and side rooms were a pipe dream in such a busy hospital.

He was permanently furious, constantly provoked, and it was taking its toll on everyone within a five-mile radius.

And now he was—despite Aled's misgivings—borderline better.

His broken arm was healed and wrapped in a soft brace to prevent any re-fracturing. His dislocated hip had faded to nothing. His ankles worked again, although they were still sore. The bruises and road rash had been eroded by the passage of time. With help, he could stand and shuffle to the bathroom, though he pitched like a drunk and almost fell back into bed every time. And this week, he'd finally stopped throwing up every time they took him for another scan or another x-ray.

But apparently, that was what he'd been waiting for.

"I can keep everything down, I don't need the catheter or the fucking bedpan anymore, all the casts are gone—I'm going home."

"Your vertigo is so severe you can't walk on your own."

"I won't be on my own."

"I have to work," Aled countered. "Come on, Gabriel. It'll just be for a few more—"

"Weeks. And no. I'm leaving *this* week."

Aled raked his hands through his hair. "You don't under—"

"No, *you* don't understand," Gabriel shot back. "Every day, it's 'good morning, Miss Gabby! How are you, Miss Gabby? When is your husband coming, Miss Gabby?' Every single fucking day. And if they open the curtains, everyone else just stares at me like I'm some kind of freak because they've all figured it out. They won't let me wear my binder because 'that's not good for you, Miss Gabby!' and the bra straps are giving me bedsores against this piece of shit pillow, and that's what I fucking feel like, Aled! I feel like shit in here. I'm not staying. I don't fucking care if I'm confined to the bed at home. I'll go to fucking Kevin's and let Judith mother me for the next six months if I have to. But I'm not staying here. So you can either help me go home, or you can get the fuck out of my way."

Aled let out a long, shaking breath.

It was show. That was all. If he refused to help, then Gabriel was stuck. The skull fracture had left him with severe vertigo, persistent migraines, and an ever-present nausea that escalated rapidly if he moved too much. And while the bone was healing nicely, one fall was all it would take to smash his head open like an egg under the wheel of a car. He would be better off here.

Physically.

But at the same time, how many times had Aled arrived for his afternoon vigils to bloodshot eyes and a hoarse voice? How often had Gabriel clung to his hand when it was time to go home? He'd heard the cheery misgendering for himself. He'd seen the contemptuous look on the doctor's face. He'd woken up in the night to lonely text messages, long rambling thoughts in the night that spilled over with torment. He'd seen the tears.

Mentally, it wasn't just Aled who was suffering.

And it hurt to say no.

"You need someone," he murmured. "You need someone there all the time. And I can't. You know I can't. And Judith's already got three kids to look after, plus the new baby when it's born..."

"I can't *do* this, Aled."

The tone wrenched at his heart, and he groaned when Gabriel buried his face in his hands.

"Gabe—"

"You don't get it," Gabriel croaked, and the first sobs had Aled up out of the chair. "You don't *get* it. It's torture. It's like being in Hackney, like my mum's spitting my deadname in my face like it'll make it fit, like I'm just this fucking *freak* who doesn't deserve to be here—"

"Oh, hey-hey-hey-hey..."

Gabriel was stiff as a board in Aled's arms. He wouldn't remove his hands. The crying shattered Aled's composure, and he tucked his nose against scratchy hair, stiff from hospital soap, and choked back a few tears of his own.

"Sweetheart, please don't do this—"

"Then get me *out* of here!"

Aled squeezed tight, but he couldn't find a way out.

Although Aled was generally monogamous, Gabriel was openly and unapologetically poly. He had three regular partners, including Aled, and a fuckbuddy for gigs. But it was Aled that he lived with all the time, not Kevin or Chris or Greg. Their house was just the two of them, and all Aled's family lived down south now. They only had Gabriel's network to help—and Gabriel's network were unavailable. His other long-term partner, Kevin, had three kids, a pregnant wife and a busy kitchen-fitting business. Gym-going Greg was a fuckbuddy, not a partner, and would be absolutely no help even if Aled could stand his ignorant presence for more than five minutes. And Aled had gone down to part-time hours until Gabriel was out of hospital, but he couldn't be around twenty-four hours a day like Gabriel would need. Gabriel had no family they could trust — nearby or otherwise. And Chris —

His brain screeched to a halt.

Chris.

Gabriel's cyclist boyfriend from Bristol. The ex-soldier with the surprisingly muscular upper body for a cardio fanatic. The most patient, placid man in the universe. The shy boyfriend of at least eighteen months now, maybe even a couple of years, who was terrified of chubby ginger marketing executive Aled purely and simply because he was a sexual dominant.

All right, he was in *Bristol*, but a single fact gleamed out of Aled's memory.

Chris hated his job.

He was always skiving off and calling in sick so he could go racing with Gabriel. He had a flatshare in some backwater village south of the city, but he always wanted to go somewhere else. He rarely insisted on Gabriel visiting him. Usually they went places together, or Chris would come up to take Aled's place when Aled had a business trip abroad. Whatever Chris' roots in the south were, they weren't all that deeply dug.

Maybe he could be persuaded.

If he could come up and play nurse while Aled was at work, then Gabriel wouldn't be left on his own. He could be forced to stay in bed. Help to get to the bathroom and take a shower. Minimise the risk of falling and killing himself. Decent food instead of tepid hospital mush. Good company, and company that wouldn't call him a woman all the time. And Chris was something of a health nut, so he was bound to make a good nurse.

Aled had never lived with one of Gabriel's other boyfriends before — hell, he'd barely spent two hours in

Chris' company in the whole time they'd been dating—but he could suck it up for a few months until Gabriel was fighting fit again. And it wouldn't take so long as it would if he stayed in the hospital or got moved out to some shoddy care home. At least at home with Chris, Gabriel would do better mentally—and probably physically, too.

If it was possible.

If Chris agreed.

"Hey."

He tightened his grip once more around Gabriel's shaking shoulders, then let go. He kissed the nasty scar and nudged the shell of Gabriel's ear with his nose.

"Let me make a phone call," he whispered. "I've got an idea. Fingers crossed, huh?"

"Will it get me out of here?"

"That's the plan."

"Okay." Gabriel's grip on his shirt eased. He looked awful, but a shaky smile shimmered around the edges of his mouth. "Who are you calling?"

"Got to ring a man about a bike."

Chapter Two

De-di-li-de, de-di-li-de, de-di-li-de-dee.

"You gonna get that?" the customer asked.

Chris slammed the faulty till drawer shut and offered a thin smile.

"Boss doesn't like us answering our phones when we're on the clock."

De-di-li-de, de-di-li-de, de-di-li-de-dee.

"Mate," the customer said, taking his change. "Your boss is a dick. And your ringtone's annoying as fuck."

"Have a nice day, sir."

The glass door clinked shut behind him, and Chris' mobile finally stopped ringing. Probably just Mum. He sighed, wishing he could sit down and check. Bob also thought sitting down behind the till was unprofessional and looked sloppy and haphazard.

Chris worked in a fucking *bike* shop. It was *meant* to look haphazard in here, for fuck's sake.

Then the shop phone started ringing, and Chris rolled his eyes. Only three people ever called the shop phone—Bob's wife, Bob's other woman and Bob's bank manager. He steeled himself for someone to scream in his ear. Two hours to go. Two hours to go. Two hours —

"Bob's Bikers, best bikes in North Somerset, Chris speaking, how can I help today?"

It was a giant run-on sentence of utter boredom, and he felt a tiny slice of his life expectancy being chipped off as he finished.

"Chris? It's Aled."

Chris' gut clenched.

"What's wrong? Is Gabriel okay?"

He was learning to hate phone calls at work. He'd take Bob's wife screaming her abuse any day over the day Aled had called and told him to get the first train to Wakefield. He still felt sick whenever the ringer started up, and Aled never called unless something was wrong.

In fact, until the day of the accident, Aled had never called him at all.

"He's fine," Aled said.

Chris let out a relieved sigh.

"Fighting to come home today."

Chris frowned. "Is he ready for that?"

"That's why I'm calling. No. But he's insistent."

Chris could imagine. Gabriel had always been so calm, placid, even playful with him. They'd never had an argument. Never shouted. Even when he was uncomfortable — usually when Chris' roommate Jack was around — he was at least polite. The worst Chris had seen was that chilly kind of politeness that southerners excelled at, betraying Gabriel's London origins. Then he'd come round in hospital, a terrifying two weeks after the accident, and lost his shit.

Loudly.

Turned out Chris was just privileged to always have him happy.

He'd religiously visited every weekend, going up on the Friday night and getting the last train home on Sunday. And every weekend since he woke up, Gabriel had been in a foul mood. He hated the food. A nurse had misgendered him and been reamed out at top volume one sunny afternoon. He hated doctors in general, without adding the long pauses before his pronouns whenever they spoke about him or the curled lip that seemed permanently affixed to the consultant's face. His head injury made him constantly nauseous and struggling with crippling vertigo, so he couldn't get out of bed or even roll over without an attack. It had taken three weeks before he could even sit up enough for a hug.

Chris had never seen him in such a bad mood...but he could understand it.

And he could definitely understand wanting to be at home instead of a hospital filled with disease, bad food and no privacy whatsoever.

"So what are you going to do?" he asked.

"He'd be better off at home," Aled said. "But the doctors are pretty clear he needs constant supervision. He can't walk on his own yet and hitting his head could be fatal at this point."

"Can't eat, either."

"Well, it's been seventy-two hours since he threw up so they're happy he can keep everything down now."

"Does it make much difference if he needs constant supervision?" Chris asked. "I mean, it's good he can, but if you can't get the time off to look after him *anyway*... Weren't your office shitty enough about all the time you took off to sit with him when he was still in critical?"

"Yeah," Aled said. "And Kevin's working and has a herd of children, Tom and Suze are down south and expecting their own, and you—"

Chris raised his eyebrows.

"Me," he said, when Aled failed to continue.

"Yeah. You."

"I have a job," Chris said stupidly.

"That you hate."

Chris cast an eye around the empty shop. Bob's Bikers was nothing more than an overpriced hobby shop kept open purely and simply by dodgy business loans. It sounded like a motorcycle place, but it didn't so much as sell L plates for scooters. Sandwiched between an accountants' firm and a dentist, it would have struggled to attract foot traffic even without the mannequin in the window that bore a strong resemblance to Chucky. Only two bikes were on display. There was next to no clothing, and the only things Chris had ever actually sold were replacement lights and inner tyre tubes. He'd sure as shit never sold an actual *bike*. He got paid minimum wage to stand here all day and stare at nothing.

Yeah, he hated it. But it paid the bills, and Chris said so.

"I'd pay," Aled said. "Free accommodation plus two hundred a week."

Fucking *hell*.

"For me to…"

"To stay at our house and look after Gabriel while I'm at work."

"Sorry," Chris said. "You're offering to pay me to look after my own boyfriend?"

"I'm offering to pay you so you can look after him and not be prevented by bills and a job you don't like."

"What does Gabriel say about this?"

Aled coughed.

"Ah. You haven't told him."

"Not...exactly."

Chris mulled it over. "How long do they think he'll need?"

"They don't know. Head injuries are unpredictable. He might have vertigo for the rest of his life, but it *has* been easing, so they're optimistic. And he hasn't had a migraine in at least a week now. But ultimately...who knows?"

That could mean anything. A few weeks. A couple of months. *Years*. What would they do if he needed help around the house for years?

"Look, it is really I come up there or he stays in the hospital?"

"Yeah."

Chris sucked in a breath. It meant ducking out of his tenancy with Jack. Quitting Bob's Bikers. Leaving Nailsea. Moving up north, albeit temporarily. And —

And what?

Watching TV with Gabriel all day? Getting to actually *see* him every day? They had a nice enough house, and the lake nearby would serve for his morning run and evening bike ride. He'd have to bring his bike and his gaming console, but even the north had internet. It wasn't *that* backward.

Probably.

It wasn't like Chris had much of a local social life. Most of his friends were other bikers around the country, or the odd gamer he'd known for a few years in the States when he'd toyed with the idea of learning to code. He came to work, he watched TV with Jack and he had Sunday dinner at Mum's. That was all he did round here.

And it would make Gabriel feel better. Probably let him heal quicker, too, without constantly stressing, and being able to sleep in his own bed. And Chris could cook. *Healthy* cook too, not whatever was causing Aled's more-than-generous spare tyre.

Gabriel would be better off at home.

"Okay," he said.

"Seriously?"

"Yeah. I'll need a few days to sort everything out here, but...yeah. I'll come up. Um. Friday. Let's say Friday, get him home for the weekend."

Aled let out a long breath. "Fuck. You're a godsend."

"I don't like seeing him in there any more than you do," Chris said. "But can you spare two hundred a week? I—"

"I'm the Head of Marketing. My boss is vice-president of the entire company. We have nine offices across the country, four in the US, two in the EU and I've been fighting tooth and nail to avoid being posted to Hong Kong to break into the Asian market. Yeah. I can spare two hundred a week."

Chris chortled. "Okay, point taken. You're rich as fuck."

"Eh. I fund Gabriel's lifestyle. You're cheap."

"Noted."

"Sort out what you need to," Aled said. "If you need a hand with anything, let me know. I'll clear out the spare room for you, and some space in the kitchen and living room. We haven't got a garage anymore, but I'll make some space in the shed for your bike. And, uh...see you...what, Thursday?"

"I'll text you," Chris said, and hung up the phone.

For a moment, he stayed right where he was, leaning against the counter. Bob was going to go spare. What was he supposed to tell his mum? He hadn't even told her Gabriel existed, or that he was in the hospital. He wasn't out. Not to Mum, not to Jack, not to Bob, not to *anyone*. He'd barely even admitted to himself that he wasn't a fucked-up version of straight, and he still wasn't entirely sold on the whole maybe-gay, maybe-asexual thing.

Then he squared his shoulders and pressed the buzzer under the desk.

Maybe it was time.

The stockroom door clicked. Bob's dirty trainers squeaked across the boards. He stopped halfway across the little shop, shamelessly adjusting himself through his grubby jeans and eyeing Chris through narrowed, watery eyes. The weak blue leaking out of the surrounding wind-burnt red looked like a watercolour painting gone horribly wrong. If he'd once been a cyclist, those days were long gone. And Chris had seen him bullshitting enough moped drivers who'd accidentally wandered in off the street to know the man had never ridden any other kind of bike in his life either.

"I need to go," Chris said.

"You what?"

"I'm quitting," he said. "I need to go. Now."

Bob blinked. A brain cell churned noisily. Then he said, "You what?" again, just for good measure.

Chris sighed and reached under the counter for his keys and phone. The shop was only a short bike ride from home. He could be back and packing before Jack got back from work.

"My partner's in hospital. He got hit by a bus, and now he needs someone to help him around the house for a few months. Which is me. So I have to go. I'm sorry, I know this leaves you in the lurch when it comes to—"

Bob frowned, scrunching those watery blues into tiny holes in his face.

"He?"

"Yeah," Chris said shortly. He ducked out from around the counter and headed for the door.

"I thought you were serious about this job," Bob called after him.

Serious?

"You pay me minimum wage to sell training wheels to nervous parents," Chris said. "I work forty hours a week here and my mum still has to top up my rent every month. So how serious do you want me to be?"

"When we get more customers through that there door—"

"And without a digital presence, it won't happen. This is *Nailsea*. You haven't got the foot traffic for any more customers."

Bob harrumphed.

"My boyfriend's in *hospital*," Chris repeated. "You could pay me forty grand a year. I'm still going."

"Hospital."

"Yeah."

"Right, so he's in good hands," Bob retorted. "I can't afford employees who run out on a shift."

Employees? Chris was the only one.

"Then dock it from my pay," Chris said. "I'm quitting either way. Here."

The itchy uniform top was gone in a heartbeat. The name badge popped off and skittered across the floor.

It bounced off Bob's filthy shoe and sat spinning like a top in front of him. Chris stalked out shirtless and marched across the road to unlock his bike from the railings outside the Chinese place.

Home.

New shirt.

Then a northbound train.

Chapter Three

"Gabby, sweetie! Your boyfriend's here to see you!"

Gabriel just grunted, not opening his eyes. The ceiling dipped and swayed like he was riding a swing whenever he looked at it, and if he looked at that cheery bitch with her Gabby this and Gabby that, he was going to throw something at her. Fuck her. Fuck the lot of them. Fuck Aled for refusing to take him home. Fuck Kevin for not answering his phone yesterday. Fuck this entire fucking system.

Fucking *fucks.*

Boots squeaked.

Gabriel frowned, but still didn't bother to look. Aled rarely wore boots. It was after lunch—he should be coming from work. And Kevin never came until the evening, thanks to the business being too busy. Maybe Greg had come? He'd only been twice—which was fine, they weren't close or anything—but in the middle of the day was a bit odd. He worked way out in Bradford.

The curtain dragged on the rail, and a weight thumped down in the chair. A heavy, hard weight. And the hand that slid into his —

Gabriel frowned and opened his eyes.

"*Chris?*"

"Hey."

"But — your train shouldn't be here for another three hours," Gabriel said stupidly.

Chris just shrugged. He lived right down near Bristol and had been coming up every Friday evening for weeks. Not by lunchtime. Gabriel didn't even know he *could* get to Wakefield by lunchtime.

"Did you take the day off?"

"Quit," he replied.

Chris didn't talk much. He was a short, shaven-headed man in his mid-twenties, plain to the point of forgettable, yet with a hard jaw and sharp eyes that added a sliver of danger. An ex-soldier, he still carried himself like a paid thug. A keen runner and cyclist, he was still as hard as a Marine, physically speaking. He'd been known to clear a room with a single frown, and God only knew what would happen if he raised his voice.

Which he didn't. He was about as dangerous as a bag of sweets. Gabriel laced their fingers together and squeezed, rubbing his thumb against a callus.

"Aled's trying to find a parking space," Chris said. "He'll be up in a minute. Um. Or twenty. It's heaving today."

"He can wait," Gabriel said sourly.

"Mm, he told me you weren't pleased."

"No kidding," Gabriel snapped, and swore when the tears started prickling at the corners of his eyes. "I've been asking every day and he keeps saying no. I want to go *home*."

"Yeah, well, what d'you think I'm here for?"

Gabriel stared. "You — what?"

The tears dissipated. His heart picked up. He mustn't have heard right. It couldn't be. Did Chris mean —

"We're taking you home."

Home.

Home.

"Oh my God," Gabriel said. "Call the nurse. Come on. Let's go. Let's go!"

No more Gabby. No more strangers wiping his fucking arse. No more shampoo that smelled like a Body Shop had thrown up on him. No more women's moisturiser for his scars. Gabriel had never cared about what moisturiser smelled like until he'd had no option but the rose-scented shit they kept smearing on him. He could have his binders back. A sports bra that wouldn't scrape against the sheets. Decent sheets!

"Come *on!*" he said.

Chris leaned over to press the bell, then opened the side cabinet and started to gather Gabriel's meagre things. He didn't have much. Some magazines, his phone, a Kindle they kept unplugging from its charger so he could never settle in for a good read. Some clothes he wasn't allowed to wear because he couldn't get them off in the bathroom by himself. The toiletries the nurses ignored.

Gabriel pushed back the sheets, wiggling his bare toes in the cool air. The dizziness clawed at him, so fierce that he couldn't sit up or swing his legs down, but who cared. They were taking him home. He'd suffer the wheelchair. Chris could even carry him once they were actually out of the hospital. He was going to be able to sleep in his own bed, eat proper food, piss in his own toilet. If he wanted to lie naked on the sofa all afternoon and bask in the early summer sun, then he could.

A nurse appeared to help, but Chris simply asked her to fetch the doctor to sign off the discharge papers, and effortlessly kept her from interfering. He wasn't a big man, but he was skilled at just getting in the way, somehow always blocking her from the cabinet or the bed or the blankets. Only when the smug wanker of a duty doctor appeared did Chris move enough to let the nurse take Gabriel's IV out, and he talked at — not to — the doctor with the same stonewalling attitude that the fat fuck had been showing Gabriel since he'd been admitted.

"I must say, I think it's too soon," the doctor said.

"Watch me give a fuck," Gabriel snapped. "Now you can get me a wheelchair and an orderly to push it, or you can get the fuck out of my way."

His things were bagged up in a plastic Tesco bag like he was homeless again. He picked at the arseless gown until Chris came to help stuff him into a T-shirt and jogging bottoms. His leg twitched weakly, still unused to movement. His back ached when he carefully sat up, and the room dipped. So did his stomach.

"Don't you dare," he muttered to it.

It settled as Chris' warm fingers rubbed his belly through the thin T-shirt. By the time Gabriel dared to open his eyes again, a flash of greying red hair caught his eye at the edges of the curtains. And thank fuck, Aled had grown a pair. He was talking at the doctor, too. Not to. Not a discussion. A one-way wash of information.

"Carry me," he said to Chris.

"What?"

"They're not getting a chair fast enough. Carry me."

"Okay."

Miraculously, a chair appeared the moment Chris' arm slid under Gabriel's legs, and he was tipped from bed to chair in a rush. His knuckles ached as he gripped the armrests, and he rolled his head to rest it against Chris' belt.

"Give me a minute."

Chris just carded his fingers through Gabriel's hair and said nothing.

Gabriel zoned out, just relaxing into the darkness of his own eyelids and the soft pass of Chris' fingers, until the chair jerked and the wheels began to move. Movement on top of vertigo was too challenging, so Gabriel didn't dare open his eyes. He felt the hospital pass by instead. The quiet hum of the corridors. The smell of coffee by the main entrance. Smokers in the shelter. Two taxi drivers in a furious argument about right of way. Engine fumes.

Freedom.

He sniffled like a little kid when he heard the beep of Aled's central locking system and clung to Chris' shoulders when he tried to lift him into the car.

"Just a minute," he mumbled. "Please."

Chris held on. Aled kissed the side of his head. For a moment, Gabriel's world narrowed to them. Their grip and their breathing and they'd finally come for him. Together. They'd finally freed him. It felt like coming out of prison.

It felt like coming out of *hell*.

"M'kay. I'm good. I'm good."

No more Gabby. No more strangers washing his genitals. No more rose-scented toiletries.

Instead, Chris' hard thighs under his head. The pine air freshener in the car. A pillow from their bed. Aled's favourite radio station. The purr as the car reversed out of the space.

They were going home.

Next door's cat sunbathing on their patio. Dawn chorus. The little old milkman coming round on Wednesday mornings like they lived in a twee cartoon. The fourth step and the way it creaked no matter where or how it was stepped on. The smell of expensive coffee and cheap toast on weekday mornings when Aled got ready for work.

Home.

Gabriel closed his eyes and relaxed in the gentle sway of the vehicle. If he couldn't see, the vertigo wasn't so bad. It felt like swinging in a hammock, even though he knew the car didn't rock *that* much.

"Thank you," he whispered.

"You can thank us by doing as you're told until you're better," Aled drawled.

"Will. Promise."

"Sure."

Gabriel smiled faintly at the scepticism.

"M'sorry for shouting at you so much."

"It's all right, sweetheart. I know you were feeling upset in there."

"Thanks for changing your mind."

"He didn't," Chris said. "I'm going to be looking after you."

"You—what?" Gabriel frowned. "There's no room in your flat. And Jack's a prick. I'm not living near his filth."

Chris chuckled. "Uh, no, genius. I'm moving into your spare room."

"You're *what*?"

"Told you. Quit my job." He tugged a lock of hair. "Aled called and said you were going mad in the hospital but you weren't ready to leave unsupervised. So I'm the supervision."

"You've moved in?"

"Yup."

His brain spun, and it wasn't anything to do with the head injury. Chris had always resisted coming north. He hated the north. Too wet, too cold, too many weird accents, and shit food. All wrong, but that was what he thought. Gabriel had been trying to persuade him to move closer for over a year and had never gotten anywhere.

"I should have tangled with that bus sooner."

Chris groaned. Aled called him a twat. Gabriel just raised a hand to curl his fingers into Chris' T-shirt, smiling loopily.

"I get *both* of you?"

"I'll have to go back to work full time," Aled warned.

"I still get both of you."

"Fine. Sure. Both of us."

"I'm dead," Gabriel announced. "I died and went to heaven, didn't I?"

"Like hell you'd get into heaven," Aled muttered.

"I heard that."

"Good, you were meant to."

The banter settled the last of his ruffled feathers from the prolonged hospital stay, and by the time Aled pulled up onto the driveway, Gabriel almost felt normal. He needed to be carried into the house, but its warmth and smell closed around him like a blanket, and the birds chattering on the feeders in the garden called to him.

"Hammock," he whispered, clinging when Chris tried to put him down on the sofa. "It's sunny, right? I want to lie in the hammock."

"Bit cool for it."

"Then get me a blanket."

Chris laughed, but lifted him again. Next door's dog barked as he stepped out of the back door into the long, thin garden that was Gabriel's domain. It wasn't carefully curated or even very pretty—ivy had eaten the back fence alive, the grass was too long, and wildflowers bobbed with fat bees all along the west side. But the hammock was wide and comfortable, the soft sway mimicking the confusion of his head injury, and he relaxed into the coarse fabric like it was the finest bed money could buy.

"You have a date," he said as Aled tucked a throw from the sofa around him.

"What?"

"You and Chris. Have a date. I'm going to nap."

Aled chuckled, kissing his hair. "Nap away. We'll sit out and enjoy a bit of sun too."

"Mind your skin, ginger biscuit."

"Piss off."

Gabriel caught the hand stroking his ribs and squeezed it.

"Thank you," he breathed. "And I'm sorry."

The next kiss touched his lips, and he opened up for it. Shallow and sweet, somehow chaste even as teeth nipped his lower lip when Aled pulled away. The sparks faded into blissful happiness, and Aled's thumb stroked his chin as though he could see them.

"Apology accepted, and you're welcome, sweetheart. Welcome home."

Gabriel drifted in the warmth of the summer sun and felt the shards of his psyche finally coming back together.

He was *home*.

Chapter Four

Gabriel hadn't been kidding about wanting a nap.

Chris carried him out to the hammock like it was their wedding day. By the time Aled picked up the pillow and throw off the sofa and followed, Gabriel was already out like a light.

"I didn't think hammocks worked that fast," Aled remarked.

"They don't. Apparently I'm a good pillow."

Aled smirked. "I'll take your word for it."

Chris flushed and looked away hastily, and Aled rolled his eyes.

"Let's do as he says. Got some ginger beer in the fridge if you fancy it?"

"Sure."

Aled left him to cool off. All those weekends sitting either side of Gabriel's bed, yet they'd never really talked to each other. Chris had always been nervous of him, and — until now — Aled hadn't been too bothered about bridging the gap. So what if Gabriel's other boyfriend was laughably afraid of him? He lived hundreds of miles away.

Only now he didn't.

Thanks to Gabriel's alcoholism, Aled didn't keep actual beer in the house — or any other type of alcohol — but he'd found ginger beer to be an acceptable alternative. He fished a couple of cans out of the fridge, along with a multipack of crisps, before heading back out and deciding to make the effort.

"I don't keep booze in the house," he said, setting down the cans. "I take it you know that rule?"

"Yeah," Chris said. "Don't drink either."

"Oh. Same —"

"No. It's bad for your liver."

"Well, here's to bowel cancer instead."

They clunked cans, and Aled stretched his feet out in the weak sun. It wasn't all that warm, but it beat hospital rooms. And the atmosphere felt warmer than it had any right to. Maybe it was Aled's good mood, or Chris' relaxation. He watched Gabriel with an absent-minded lack of focus, rather than keeping one eye firmly on Aled.

"Reckon he'll go to bed early tonight?"

"Yeah," Aled said.

"Mind if I hook up my games console?"

"In the spare room?"

"Uh, I mean, I *can* —"

"No, you can't," Aled said. "It's bust. Use the living room."

"Thanks."

"You much of a gamer?"

Chris shrugged. "I guess. I game more than I watch telly. I only watch comedy stand-up on TV, really."

"Let me guess. You're a Russell Howard fan."

"Fuck off!"

Aled laughed at the vehement response. "Sorry, sorry. Figured you preferred that nicer brand of comedy."

Chris snorted. "I do, but not *that* placid."

"Who's your favourite, then?"

They argued good-naturedly. They could agree on Josh Widdecombe being shite, but were divided on Jimmy Carr. Chris refused to admit anything about Bill Bailey, but did admit to watching everything Dylan Moran had ever done, his one exception to a pattern of not bothering with TV shows featuring comedians.

"I haven't watched comedy TV in years," Aled admitted to that one "Gabriel would kill me, but I miss Frankie Boyle."

"You would. Bloody northern gingers."

"He's Scottish, you twat."

"You're all foreigners north of Birmingham."

Aled laughed.

"I've got *Black Books* on a pen drive somewhere if you want to watch it once Gabriel's gone to bed this evening. He thinks it's boring, so we might as well take our chance."

"Surprised he doesn't find me boring," Chris said.

"He's mad about you."

"Yeah. And you know what else he's mad for? Sex."

"Uh, *yeah*, I know that part."

Chris coughed a bitter laugh.

"Gabriel's the first person I ever fucked and liked it."

Aled threw him a look. "You what?"

"I hate it," Chris said. "I only do it because the frustration is even worse. But with Gabriel, it's okay."

"Er. Good? How the fuck have you been fucking?"

The coarseness didn't seem bother Chris.

"Ace. Probably. Remember?"

"What?"

"Asexual." He shifted to dump the empty can on the table. "Probably." He dropped his hands between his knees and fidgeted.

"If you hate sex, where's the probably?"

"'Cause I have to sometimes."

"Yeah but it's about who you want to fuck, isn't it? Not whether you want to fuck at all. I mean—" Aled waved a hand. "I didn't sleep with a man until I was in my twenties, but I was still a bisexual teenager, 'cause I still looked at some guys like…hell yeah, I would."

Chris wrinkled his nose. "I guess."

"So you're ace with a sex drive. That's gotta suck."

"Yeah."

"What d'you even do?" Aled asked. "I mean, he's kinky as fuck."

Chris considered the grass between his shoes.

"You ever—" He cleared his throat. "You ever think you're fucked up for what you like?"

Aled snorted. "Welcome to my life."

"Yeah?"

"I get off on him begging me not to hurt him. Yeah. I know what it's like."

He'd spent years worrying about that. *Years.* He'd grown up wondering when he'd snap and go to prison. When he'd finally go crazy and rape someone. When the line between fantasy and reality would finally be erased.

And it hadn't.

His games with Gabriel were coercive, controlling, sometimes violent—and ended abruptly at the utterance of a safe word. They cuddled on the sofa. They went out to eat on special occasions. There were limits he'd never crossed, both his limits and Gabriel's. He was thirty-six, and yet to cross the line.

So maybe he never would.

"Sometimes he rides me and we talk and it's like we're not having sex at all," Chris said. "Like he'll just — sit on me and...and yeah."

He shuddered like something was crawling under his skin.

"Huh," Aled said.

"I don't think he likes it much either, but he does it then it's over and I can just forget about it for a while."

He fidgeted with the knee of his jeans.

"Then sometimes — "

He trailed off. Aled waited. He remembered this part. The agony of finally opening up to someone. For him, it had been his best friend. But for Chris...perhaps there was nobody else to open up *to*. Or perhaps he found some safety in admitting things to Aled, a man who clearly had much more dangerous fantasies than being ridden.

"Sometimes I fuck him while he's asleep."

Aled suppressed the flinch.

Subs had limits, but so did doms. And that was one of Aled's. Whatever they did, he had to be one hundred percent sure Gabriel was capable of removing consent, right then and right there. So he'd never played with drugs. Never fucked Gabriel in his sleep. Never so much as wanked off when he was dozing in the same bed. He couldn't. Whatever limits he could put in place when they were both awake and aware were wiped out by sleep — no matter how many times Gabriel had tried to give him permission.

Aled knew it was just one of his things. Kevin played with sedatives now and then. Gabriel had mentioned sleep sex with Chris on occasion. But once Aled had explained his reasons, Gabriel had never asked him again, and Aled had appreciated the fake ignorance and the lack of talking about it. If Aled couldn't use knives, Gabriel couldn't be out of it.

But he knew Chris had permission and crushed the urge to shrink away as Chris kept talking.

"If I'm allowed, he'll come to bed naked and I can just —"

Chris' hands were shaking.

"Hey," Aled interrupted. "It's all right."

"Is it?" Chris croaked.

"Yeah. 'Cause you've got permission. That's what makes it all right. S'that easy."

Chris kept leaning forward until his elbows were on his knees and his head dangled limply down. Aled placed a hand on his shoulder, wondering if he was going to faint.

"You all right?"

"That easy," Chris croaked.

"Yup."

"Easy."

"Yup. Do you wear a rubber?"

"Yeah."

"Bet he likes trying to figure it out in the morning."

Chris flashed him a weak smile. "Yeah."

"One of his kinks, the sleep thing," Aled said. "I can't do it. Can do almost anything if I can get a safeword out of him, but asleep? No chance. That'd set off all my issues no matter how much he liked it."

"It's okay if — if they're not responding. Like it's…a better type of wanking or something."

He visibly cringed at how it sounded, and Aled decided to leave that one be.

"Explains one thing," he remarked instead.

"What?"

"When he comes back from a trip with you, he usually wants something *savage*," Aled said. "He gets like that if he's had sex but not an orgasm. Guess I never put two and two together. Thanks."

"Thanks?" Chris echoed.

"Yeah. Some of our best games were probably because of you."

Chris' smile was wobbly, and he dropped it quickly.

"Don't worry about it," Aled said. "You've got permission to do it. And he's no pushover with his consent."

"I wouldn't know," Chris confessed. "He's never tried to stop me."

Aled laughed. "Well, take it from the man who's been safeworded halfway through an orgasm—he's no pushover with his consent."

Chris blinked. "What the hell were you doing halfway through an orgasm?"

"You don't want to know, but he didn't like it," Aled chuckled, lifting his can to his lips. He figured that telling Chris he'd threatened to rip Gabriel's nipple off with a staple remover for calling him a rapist would be a bit much for their fledgling friendship.

"When did you accept your sex life?"

"Eh?"

"What you like to do. You know. The violence."

"Oh. Early twenties. My wife was a big help." Christ, he hadn't thought about his ex-wife in ages. "She was a real powerhouse in every other aspect of her life, but she had some really intense sex fantasies. That's what I liked about her, to be honest. I knew she wanted me to do everything I was doing in the bedroom because she'd murder me if I so much as left a pair of dirty socks on the floor the rest of the time. Gabriel does the same. I can trust him, because he's happy to rip me a new one if I'm doing something he doesn't like, sexually or otherwise. So if he's letting you do it, then either he doesn't give a damn or he likes it. And" — Aled raised his can in a 'cheers' gesture — "from the man who fucks him after you're done with him, I'm going to say he likes it."

"He doesn't even get off. Why would he like it?"

"I don't know why he likes being fisted either, but he does."

"He likes *what*?"

Aled laughed.

"You fist him? How does it even fit?"

"I don't use his arse, for one."

"Even then!"

"In theory, a baby can come out of there. My fist is nowhere near the size of a baby's head."

"Yeah but your fist is going *in*. Not out. I've taken dumps bigger than your fist, and it still wouldn't fit going up there."

Aled buckled with laughter. He'd thought he'd have to get Chris drunk to talk about sex, but if it all it took was a ginger beer and some sunshine, what the hell *would* booze get out of him?

"What's your favourite thing?" Chris asked, cracking open another can.

"Sex-wise?"

"Yeah. I mean, you do like everything with him, but what's your favourite thing ever?"

"With Gabriel, or *ever*?"

"Gabriel."

Matthew J. Metzger

Aled hummed. He leaned back, propping his half-empty can on his stomach. He didn't feel especially sexual—oversized gut, rumpled hair, glasses almost hanging off the end of his nose. But it lurked just under the surface as always, and he dragged up the memory like it had only been yesterday.

"When he still lived in Belle Isle, we played this game once. We pretended he owed me money, so I locked him in his flat until he paid it off."

"With sex?"

"Bingo. Either he went out and whored himself for the money, or he fucked me for free until it would have cost me that much to hire someone. Kept him gagged so he couldn't get help and locked him in his bathroom while I was out so he couldn't get out the windows. When he had to go to work, I'd plug him and put him in a chastity belt—he didn't like that so much—and drop him off and pick him up after. We played for three days before it got a bit too real for me and I stopped it."

"You ever done it since?"

"Variations," Aled said. "He's a bit more sensitive about money so we don't tend to do that part anymore. And he refuses to play at all at his new job. Likes it too much to risk it. But occasionally I buy him off Kevin and keep him for a weekend like a toy."

Chris hummed. "So—what about ever?"

"Huh?"

"You asked if I meant with Gabriel or ever."

"Ah. Knife play."

Chris cringed. "Oh hell no."

"Yeah, that's his reaction." Aled grinned. "I don't know. There's something about it. Especially on pale skin. But he'll never let me, and it's just a nice fantasy.

I don't *need* it, and it's not worth finding a second sub for. So I've not done it in years."

Chris finally sat back and stretched.

"Thanks."

"For what?"

"Just—talking about this shit with me."

"No problem."

"I'm going for a run before dinner. Though here's an idea. For your old toy game."

"I'm listening."

"Well, he's going to need loads of running up and down to the hospital, and physio and taking care of, right?"

"Kind of why you're here, isn't it?"

"Sure. But you're paying. Maybe he should be."

The idea flashed through his head like lightning, and Aled smirked. Chris blinked, then hastily excused himself.

"Guess you don't need to be sexual to have good sexual ideas," Aled yelled after him.

"Uh. Guess not!"

"Well, if those are the ideas you come up with, Chris, then we can talk about sex any time you want. Have a good run."

Aled eyed the sleeping body in the hammock as Chris disappeared into the house, and rubbed his bristling jaw thoughtfully.

"You said your southern biker boyfriend was a shy little sweetheart," he mused. "I think maybe we can pull him out of his shell a little more. What do you say, angel?"

Gabriel, of course, said nothing.

For now.

Chapter Five

Chris stepped out of the shower and paused.

He'd stayed the night at Gabriel's before, but only once or twice with Aled in the house. And those one or two times had always been with the same expectation – one or other of them would be gone by the morning.

But he could hear Aled talking to someone on the phone downstairs.

He'd still be there on Saturday morning. And Sunday. He'd go to work on Monday, then come back in the afternoon. And Tuesday. And so on and so forth.

He'd be *around*.

Chris really wasn't used to Aled being around, and he felt paralysed by it. Stupidly so. Of course he'd known that would be how it worked, but –

But.

He dried off in the bathroom, turning his jumbled thoughts over in his head. The spare room would be *his* room. Properly his. No swapping it for the master bedroom once Aled had gone. It wasn't a temporary stopping point like it had been before. He'd sleep there every night, with Aled and Gabriel cuddled up together just the other side of the wall.

To his surprise, a flicker of jealousy sparked up in his chest.

Why?

Why should he be relegated to the spare room, and Aled to the master bed? Weren't they both Gabriel's boyfriends? Didn't he love them both? Chris wasn't here for the short term. Why should he have to take the spare room all the time? Why couldn't he and Aled switch sometimes?

Chris snuffed it out as quickly as it had arrived, and stepped into his boxers. He was being stupid. Gabriel was ill. It wasn't like he'd moved in for fun.

He stepped out onto the landing in his boxers and slippers, still drying off his chest. Gabriel whistled from the master bedroom and Chris paused in the doorway, raising his eyebrows at the tired smile thrown at him.

"C'mon," Gabriel said, patting the bed. "Watch this with me."

"It's half ten. I'm calling it a day," Chris said.

"Exactly."

Chris blinked. "Um. No, I'm—I'm in the guest room."

Gabriel frowned muzzily. He'd had his painkillers with dinner, and if the vertigo made him a little loopy, the painkillers finished him off.

"But you're not a guest," he said.

"This is your room. With Aled. That's mine."

"No. This is my bed. For me an' my boyfriends. So come *here*."

Chris laughed. "Right, because me and Aled are going to share a bed."

"Didn't your garden date go well?"

"We had a couple of ginger beers and a chat," Chris said. "Hardly a date."

"You were one-on-one and the idea was to get to know each other, right? That's a date," Gabriel countered.

"God, you're impossible."

"Says the man just standing there. C'mon. Come cuddle me."

Chris sighed and inched into the room. It was a hedonist's wet dream. Thick carpet, silk lining the ceiling to mimic a tent canopy, soft lights, a bed that could drown a man and a TV the size of a small cinema screen. Sprawled out in the middle of the bed, Gabriel looked like he was on a luxury holiday.

"Aled will be up soon."

"Yeah, so? C'mon."

"You really want me to sleep in here with the two of you."

"*Yes*, you idiot. C'mon."

Chris groaned, and stepped out to dump his towel back in his room. Fine. If Gabriel wanted to get him killed, so be it. It might teach the flirt a lesson.

The bed was a king size, and it was probably just as well. Chris was able to slide into the far side without disturbing Gabriel's middle-of-the-pillows position too much and tucked his hands behind his head so Gabriel could perform his usual trick of using Chris' armpit like a pillow. The mattress was deeper than he remembered. This was going to be like getting drugged to sleep.

"So what are we falling asleep to?"

"This murder documentary."

"Why?"

"Why not?"

Chris screwed up his face as a mutilated corpse flashed up on the screen. "Gross."

"Oh, they were just saying that the killer kept dumping them out in the desert so they'd rot faster."

"Why are you like this?" Chris complained.

Gabriel chuckled and poked his foot under the covers. "Ssh. I wanna hear how the insects helped solve it."

Chris shut up, grimacing at the screen every now and then and trying not to track Aled pacing around downstairs. When the phone call stopped, a knot formed in the pit of Chris' stomach. When the stairs creaked, a sweat broke out on his back.

Then Aled said, "Joining us?" and tossed his shirt into the laundry hamper as he walked through the door.

"Apparently."

"I nagged," Gabriel admitted with a huge yawn. "Who was that?"

"Imogen from work."

"Something come up?"

"Nah, just bitching about a mutually loathed twassock."

Chris breathed in tiny increments. Aled was just...ignoring him. Undressing down to his briefs. Wandering out to brush his teeth. Coming back scratching his hairy belly like they'd all been married for years. The bed dipped as he climbed in, and he leaned over to kiss Gabriel's cheek, and —

That was it.

He lay down on Gabriel's other side, a hand on the flat belly separating him from Chris, and closed his eyes. Gabriel turned the volume down. A forensic scientist was talking about flies. A low snore emanated from the other side of the bed.

And the knot in Chris' stomach dissolved.

"You shouldn't be so scared all the time," Gabriel murmured.

"You take some getting used to."

"You've slept in a bed with me loads of times. *Aled* is what you're getting used to."

"Yeah, yeah, whatever."

They watched the rest of the documentary in silence. Gabriel dozed off as they started talking about the trial, and Chris turned it off once the credits rolled. The bedroom darkened. A few final birds twittered outside. A cat began singing on the back fence. In the distance, he could faintly hear motorway traffic, a light breeze carrying the noise over the fields and gentle hills.

But sleep eluded him.

Aled was breathing deep and slow on the other side of the bed, oblivious to the world. Gabriel had rolled onto his side and tucked his bum against Chris' hip. On their own, Chris would have turned over and taken up the sleeping invitation for a spoon.

But Aled—

Chris closed his eyes and gave himself a talking to. Aled had invited him here. Aled had seen him kiss Gabriel at the hospital. Aled *knew*. For fuck's sake, what was Chris worrying about?

Slowly, he rotated his hips. Chest. Drew up his legs. Slid his arm over Gabriel's waist.

Gabriel mumbled something and tucked up his knees towards his chest. A hand twitched. His ribs pushed lightly at the underside of Chris' arm.

And nothing happened.

Chris exhaled heavily into Gabriel's hair and tried to relax. So he was supposed to sleep here at night. Great. That was fine. Gabriel would stay in the middle and separate him from Aled, and it would be fine. Comfortable. Sensible, too, if he was playing nurse.

It would be fine.

And he'd keep telling himself that until he believed it.

* * * *

Chris woke with the dawn.

The chorus was part of the reason for it. He was used to a bit of chatter in Nailsea, but Newmillerdam was like Glastonbury For Birds was going off outside the window. When one hit the window with a deafening smack, neither Aled nor Gabriel twitched.

Slowly, Chris drew back his arm.

He was still cuddled up to Gabriel's back. They'd all contracted in the night—Gabriel's face was buried in Aled's armpit, and Aled was flat on his back, one arm over his head and his mouth twisted open in a silent snore. His eyes looked small and weak without his glasses, and there were grey hairs in his eyebrows. He looked older. Blander. Less—

"Huh," Chris said.

He'd never looked less like a sadistic dominant.

Chris didn't feel like chancing it, though, and slipped free of the bed. His skin was sticky hot, and he snuck out to find his bag and slip back into the bathroom. A quick rinse off and a pair of shorts was all he needed. He refilled his water bottle at the kitchen sink, laced his trainers by the door and borrowed

Gabriel's house keys to let himself out into the noisy morning.

The first hundred yards swept all the thoughts away.

Gabriel laughed at him and called him a fitness freak, but it wasn't about washboard abs and weightlifting to Chris. It was about the shutdown. When the brain was too busy breathing, putting one foot in front of the other, remembering to drink, watching out for stitches, minding the rabbit holes in the bank, to *think*. When the busy nature of life had to stop, because it couldn't be done alongside the air raking through his lungs or the pounding pressure of his heart.

He couldn't worry about his weird sex life. About his lack of social circle. About coming out to his mum. About Aled.

When he ran—or raced, or swam, or hiked—there was nothing but his physical being and nature. Birds didn't care if he liked to fuck. The glittering lake didn't have shit opinions.

Nature was the bedrock of his relationship with Gabriel, truth be told. They'd met at a cycling event, and Chris had been riding the endorphin high when he'd asked him out. If his brain had been online, he'd never have done it. Too scared. Too confused. But he had, because of the buzz. And their first date had been another ride and benefited from much the same effect. He'd kept himself too wired to ask himself any questions.

If he'd asked, he'd have talked himself out of it.

So he adopted the same tactic, and hoped it would work once more. He didn't need to ask how he stood with Aled. He wasn't attracted to Aled. Aled probably wasn't attracted to him. They just had Gabriel in common, and that was all they needed. He had to relax.

At the completion of the lap round the water, Chris wondered if that wasn't asking a little much of his anxiety-riddled brain.

But that was a thought.

So he set off for another lap.

Chapter Six

For the first time in weeks, Gabriel felt like he'd slept *properly*.

No nurses fussing about in the night. No beeps and clicks. No breakfast at half seven whether he wanted to get up yet or not. No hard mattress digging into his spine and no itchy sheets aggravating his skin. No drips and catheters to stop him from —

Wait.

Halfway through turning over, Gabriel froze up as the room — and his stomach — rolled. He closed his eyes, but it didn't do much to help. The bed was sliding under him. He was going to fall. It was crazy and he knew it, but — but —

He was going to fall.

"Aled!"

He clung to the sheets until his knuckles ached. Muscles shuddered. The bed had to be flat, must be flat, couldn't be anything except flat...

The door creaked.

"What's up?"

"M'falling. M'falling!"

Feet padded across the carpet. Aled's voice was soft, but his hands were firm on Gabriel's back and shoulder.

"No, you're not."

"I know, I know, but I am —"

"No. You're not."

The duvet shifted. The mattress dipped violently and Gabriel burst into humiliating tears as the terror sank cold claws into his brain.

Then —

Aled's body settled against his back. Between him and the floor. His biceps slid under Gabriel's head until the rhythm of his heart beat against Gabriel's ear. His other arm locked tight around Gabriel's waist. Holding on. Anchoring him.

The bed was still tipped at a steep angle, but Aled lay against his back, and Aled wasn't falling.

"Better?"

"Mm."

He carefully let go of the sheets with one hand. His fingers shook as he scrubbed the tears away, face burning with embarrassment.

"Thanks," he whispered.

"S'fine."

"Think — think you might be stuck now."

Aled chuckled deeply. "Well, there's always the TV."

Gabriel pushed his nose against Aled's arm and inhaled. He smelled of toast and the nice aftershave. His arm hair tickled Gabriel's cheek. He was wearing pyjamas, the worn fabric familiar against Gabriel's skin. The bed was a rumpled mess, all flowing lines and soft cotton sliding through Gabriel's fingers, but Aled was solid as a rock.

Well, a soft rock.

Clay.

"Where's Chris?"

"Shower. Just got back from his run. His two-hour run."

"Oh."

"Oh? He does that often?"

"Every day."

"*Fuck* that," Aled said emphatically. "What a health freak."

Gabriel laughed weakly as the humour began to dig in where the illogical fear had gripped him.

"I'm sure he'd let you join him…"

"No chance."

It was the first time since the accident that Aled had sounded really normal, and Gabriel squeezed his wrist. He'd been just as messy as Gabriel in the hospital. Not going home, living off vending machines, barely sleeping, taking all of Gabriel's abuse about the situation. It had been hell for the both of them, and an entirely different embarrassment burned on Gabriel's tongue.

"I'm sorry."

"For what?"

"For being a dick. Shouting at you all the time and being so angry."

Aled squeezed gently. "It's all right, darling."

"It's not—"

"Maybe not, but it's understandable. You were in pain and they were making it worse with their transphobic crap. But you're home now, so no more bullshit. I'll only take extreme pain for an excuse. Deal?"

Gabriel laughed shakily. "Deal."

It had been a shock to the system. He was used to the odd transphobic troll on Grindr or FetLife, but his facial scruff and small tits meant it had been years since anyone had been a dick to him about his gender in person, to his face, in his physical space. And he'd not only forgotten how it felt, but how to deal with it. It had been like ripping open the wounds his family had gouged into his skin, and bleeding anew all over the floor.

Now he was home, held fast in Aled's arms, where he was nothing but *Gabriel*. Not 'Miss Lazarri' or 'Gabby' or 'stupid dyke' or 'ungrateful bitch'.

Just Gabriel.

"I used to be angry every day," he whispered. "Back before—before Kevin and you and Chris and Greg and even Michael."

Aled made a low grumbling noise at the mention of Gabriel's ex.

"That was every day."

"Yeah, well, now it's a blip," Aled said. He kissed the back of Gabriel's head. "In other news, hurry up and grow this out. I miss your hair."

"Me too."

"And that scar can do with being hidden."

"Oh, I don't mind it," Gabriel said. He wriggled a little, settling against Aled's soft belly. "You know what you should do?"

"What?"

"Have a self-care day."

"Have a what now?"

"Like—" He thought. Aled's way of relaxing was usually violent sex, which was out of the question for obvious reasons, or the gym. He was a keen swimmer, and even keener on the little sauna and spa pool at his leisure centre of choice, but he hadn't been since that bus had wrecked Gabriel's bike. And brain.

"Maybe once Chris is done in the bathroom, he can come here and you can swap?"

"Swap?"

"Yeah. You can go swimming and lounge around in the spa pool after."

Aled chuckled. A bristly kiss nudged the back of Gabriel's ear, and he readied himself for a row.

Only for Aled to say, "Sounds like a good idea."

That was a surprise. "Yeah?"

"Mm. Give you and Chris a bit of alone time and give me a bit of rest and relaxation. I slept like the dead last night, now you're finally back where you belong."

"Semi-naked in bed?"

"Semi-naked at *home*. Bed is optional."

Gabriel snorted. "Not right now it's not. I'm going to need carrying to the toilet later."

"Well, Chris can definitely help with that. I'll put my back out."

"You calling me fat?"

"After what you refused to eat in hospital? If anything, you could stand to gain a few."

"Good answer. Get me a McDonalds on your way home from the pool."

"Pretty sure your health-nut boyfriend won't like that."

The bathroom door opened.

"Speak of the devil," Aled said.

"What?" Chris called as he padded into the spare room.

"Hey!" Gabriel objected. "You live in here now!"

"My boxers live in here!"

"Move them!"

Chris reappeared in the bedroom doorway in his boxers, towelling his head and shoulders dry. He was a fine specimen, and not for the first time, Gabriel mourned his total lack of interest in sex. Imagine getting drilled by *that*. Ugh, yes please.

"We reached a deal," Gabriel said. "You need to come here where Aled is, then he's going to go out and get wet."

"Er. Excuse me?"

"I'm going swimming," Aled said, and patted Gabriel's chest. "And this one is having a vertigo attack."

"Oh. *Oh*! Okay. Hang on. Let me get some snacks and set up the TV. We can start on a box set or something."

"Be very careful what you pick from downstairs!" Gabriel yelled after him, then grinned when Aled sniggered against his ear. "What? I'm up for a bit of porn but he wouldn't like it."

"I put it away," Aled said.

"Spoilsport."

"Hey, we need him. Don't upset him."

"He's not that easy to upset."

Much easier to upset was Gabriel's stomach. Although he hadn't actually been sick in several days, the nausea was still intensely powerful. When Chris and Aled eventually swapped, Gabriel just buried his face in a pillow and tried to ward off both the terrifying sensation of falling from a thousand feet, and the punch of his stomach trying to turn itself inside out.

Then Chris' chest pressed up against his back, and hairy legs tangled with his own.

"There you go. I've got you."

His hand was bigger than Aled's, and firm on Gabriel's jumping belly. It soothed him at once. The soft music of a DVD root menu drew him back from the dizzy edge, and he eventually relaxed enough to nod once, and listen to it cut out in favour of dramatic opening music.

"What are we watching?"

"Figured we could mock some of the DC movies."

"*Batman* and *X-Men* and all that?"

"Yep."

"Are they bad?"

"Mostly, though there's a couple of gems."

"M'kay." That was permission to make fun of them. Nerds like Aled and Chris could get so *uptight* sometimes. "Where's Aled?"

"Already gone. You zoned out for a little bit there."

"Urgh, no kidding. I want this to be over."

Chris kissed his hair, much like Aled had.

"I know, but you'll get there," he promised. "You want to try lying on your back so you can watch this instead of listen?"

It took a little effort, and a long period of just lying there with his face tucked into Chris' shoulder to ward off the crippling dizziness, but it didn't feel so scary as it had in the hospital. Aled had held him. And now Chris was holding him. There was a bad film to watch, and later Chris would help him to the bathroom and it wouldn't feel humiliating like it had in the ward with strangers. When Aled came back, he'd make lunch.

Maybe they'd swap back, or maybe all three of them would sit up against the pillows and watch the movie, Gabriel bracketed by his boyfriends.

"Chris?"

"Mm."

"Thanks for coming."

Chris scratched the back of his neck lightly as though he were a cat. "S'fine."

"I mean, I know Aled's paying you to, but—"

"That's purely so I can afford to do it," Chris said. "I've got to eat and pay off my credit cards too."

"I know. But thanks. I needed you—both of you—and you came for me. I know it sounds really over the top and dramatic, but I feel like you rescued me yesterday."

Chris kissed the top of his head.

"So thanks for being here."

"Thanks for not letting the bus win," Chris murmured.

"I don't remember it," Gabriel admitted. "I was at work then I was in hospital. I don't remember anything about the accident."

It was probably a good thing. Aled had told him that his helmet and bike had both been totalled beyond repair. He'd seen the original x-rays of his forearm and the nasty breaks that had now, thankfully, healed. And the bubbling scar of road rash all up one leg said he'd either skidded or been dragged by something.

But he didn't remember.

He didn't even really know if it had been a close thing or just looked dramatic because of the shaved head and the stitches. The doctors had done their level best not to tell him anything, and by the time he'd been up to asking Aled, it was obvious he would eventually be all right.

Lying there with Chris, he toyed with the idea of asking—but then filed it away. It was too soon. They were both a little jumpy, and Gabriel wanted to just enjoy being home again.

"Chris?"

"Mm?"

"After the movie, can you help me in the shower?"

"Sure."

"For, like…forty minutes."

"Sorry?"

"I want a *long* shower."

"Sure you just don't want a bath?" Chris asked.

"You can lift me in and out of the bath?"

"Sure."

Gabriel grinned. "*Really*?"

"Yeah. I should know. Jack's fallen in the tub drunk enough times, and you don't weigh as much as he does. If you shut up and watch the film, I'll help you have a bath."

A long soak in the bath sounded like heaven, even if it would set off the vertigo like crazy.

"Deal," Gabriel said.

And nothing was going to smell like roses.

Chapter Seven

Aled went back to full-time work on Monday.

It was a necessary evil. He'd been fighting to stay part-time long enough to get Gabriel home, especially as — given as how they weren't married — HR didn't regard Gabriel as family, and certainly not as a dependant. And there was only so much his boss could do against the inhumanity of Human Resources. It was a relief not to have to argue with them anymore, even if he took twice as long getting ready as usual and had to be shouted out of the door.

"The quicker you go, the quicker you can come back!" Gabriel had bellowed down the stairs, and Aled left to spare the neighbours more grief.

It felt…odd.

Certainly better than being at work while Gabriel was in the hospital, but the sustained period between driving into Leeds and getting to drive back out again felt strange. He was itching to send a text by the time he pulled into the car park, but resisted the urge. If he was good and didn't fuss, Gabriel was more likely to be in a cuddly mood when he got home. Anyway, he'd be fine. He had Chris to himself all day. There was nothing to worry about.

Which had never stopped anyone on the planet from worrying about anything, but it was worth a shot.

Instead, Aled decided to check in to a different part of his life. Waving to the security guard on the front desk as he swiped into the building, he took the stairs for a little exercise then settled into his all-window fishbowl of an office by littering his desk with papers, firing up the computer and picking up the phone.

Starting with nine for an outside line and following it with a Penzance area code.

A bored woman answered at once. In the background, a TV chattered too loudly and a knife was slamming through some kind of foodstuff onto a chopping block with annoyed force. "Suze speaking." In two words, she said loud and clear that she wasn't in the mood for any telemarketing shit.

"Hey, Suze, it's me."

Her tone lifted at once. "Aled! How's everything going? How's Gabriel?"

"Home," Aled said. "We took him home on Friday."

"We?"

"Me and Chris."

"His Birmingham guy?"

"Bristol."

"Whatever," she said. "So he's — wait, he's staying to help out? I mean…you're ringing on a withheld number, so…"

"So I'm at work, yeah."

"Ohhh," she said. "I got it. So he's moved up to help out while you're working?"

"Yeah," Aled said. "I said I'd cover his expenses and pay him a bit, and he jacked in his crap job and got the next train north."

"That's a good solution. Is it working? How's he doing? Gabriel, I mean."

"Better already," Aled admitted. "The mood change is incredible. He looks better, he sounds better, he — Christ. The *difference*. All because of that shitty misgendering crap from the hospital. You'd think after all these years, I'd understand how his gender works better than I do."

Aled was as cisgender as cisgender came, but sometimes his own ignorance frustrated him. He figured he knew it all, but then he'd still get surprised by bullshit like the hospital. Every now and then, he'd wonder why Gabriel put the fuck up with having such a dumbshit for a dominant.

"You understood enough to get him out of there," Suze consoled. "Don't beat yourself up too hard. Has he forgiven you?"

"Yeah. And apologised for being a dick."

"There you go. Move on. So he's doing better at home?"

"Yeah." Aled leaned back in his chair with a long sigh. "He's not had any migraines yet, or been sick, but the nausea is still quite rough and he's got this crippling vertigo. He can barely walk. He had a panic attack on Saturday morning because he thought he was going to fall off the bed when he was lying down."

"Oh, the poor thing…"

"But he's behaving. Sleeps a lot, or watches TV. And he's eating better than he did in the hospital."

The food hadn't actually been too bad, if a little carb-heavy for a man who wasn't able to move, but Gabriel had vehemently disagreed. He'd even got health nut Chris smuggling in KFCs from the outside world. When he'd not even raised a sardonic eyebrow at the vegetarian chilli Chris had made on Sunday night, Aled had felt a knot he didn't know he had unlock inside his chest.

"Bless him," Suze said. "Tom's like that with hospitals. You remember when he broke his ankle in university? Four days and he wouldn't touch a thing."

"I think it's come on a bit since then."

"You're so cute when you're optimistic."

Aled laughed, then the confession rushed out of him. "It's so good to have him home."

"Of course it is!" Suze said. "You were worrying yourself into an early grave. How are *you* doing?"

"I just—fuck, I've *slept*, Suze. I've slept properly. I went to the pool on Saturday and spent an hour in the spa pool."

He felt human. Alive. *Properly* alive, too, not just going through the numb motions. It had been weeks—months—since he'd felt like a human being, much less someone's friend or partner. The phone call from the hospital right after the accident had sucked all the sensation out of him, and it had only crept back in this weekend, with Gabriel home where he belonged.

"I feel like I did after I finally accepted my divorce. Like I've been dead on the inside and it's over now," he said. "I feel like *me* again."

"Oh, honey. You should have taken the week off," Suze said. "Stayed at home and recovered along with him."

Aled snorted. "Arthur would have let me, but the board are being right awkward sods about it. Oh hey, I forgot to tell you. I'm out at work now."

"Because of all this?"

"Yep."

"Congratulations…I think."

"Yeah," Aled said sourly. "Arthur's fine—you know what he's like, couldn't give a toss if I ate babies for breakfast—but there's been the odd funny look in meetings. Milligan's made a crass remark or two. Stupid old fucks."

Movement flickered at the door. His secretary waved papers through the window, and he beckoned her in.

"One second, Gerald," he said in an officious tone, then covered the mouthpiece. "Yes?"

"Sorry to disturb you, Mr Evans, but Mr Mitchell just dropped off the budget reports and said you'd need to see them today before they get signed off this afternoon."

"I'll take a look. Thank you."

"Coffee?"

"Not just yet." He waggled the phone and whispered. "Bit of a sensitive juggling act."

"Ah! Well, buzz me when you're done and I'll bring you a brew."

"You're an angel."

She flitted back out, and he uncovered the phone.

"Sorry. Secretary alert."

"No worries. I figured. So the board are homophobic?"

"Are you surprised?"

"Nah. Especially not about Milligan. Remember the fight he put up when the staff union wanted to put a rainbow flag up in the lobby for pride month? Fuck 'em," Suze said. "Quit. Move to Cornwall and take up selling rock to tourists."

Aled laughed. "I wish."

"I'm just saying, Tom's got his eye on expanding the business and he'll need marketing experts to pull it off…"

"Call me when he's offering my salary."

"Greedy fuck."

"Hey, I'm supporting three people on this wage, and my partner's boyfriend eats a lot more than a new baby. Speaking of which—"

"Still nothing," Suze said mournfully. "Due next week." Then her voice dropped. "Promise to keep it a secret?"

"Uh. Sure?"

"*Promise.* I've not even told Tom."

Aled smirked. Much as Suze and Tom had a perfectly happy marriage and were well-suited, Aled knew a *lot* of things that Tom didn't. His place as the brother and best friend had never been usurped by Suze's affable oaf of a partner, and going by their married track record, never would be.

"Okay, I promise."

"So you know he missed the second scan because of that traffic accident that got him stuck on the road for six hours and he ended up totalling his car by trying to drive it across some fields?"

"Yeah."

"Well, I kind of…told a little white lie."

"About what?"

"His mum *really* wants a granddaughter, so we were going to ask at the scan and find out. But it's *Brenda*, you know? So I said the midwife couldn't tell, but she *could*."

"So? Is it a girl?"

"*Nope*," Suze said in the most gleeful tone Aled had ever heard. He laughed. "Going to have a little boy. When he feels like showing up, that is."

"Well, congratulations," he said. He'd never really understood or cared about boys versus girls, or even having children in general, but Suze didn't particularly like her overbearing mother-in-law so he could appreciate her satisfaction. "Why didn't you tell Tom?"

"He'd be so giddy he'd never keep it secret," she said. "He wants both so he won't mind which comes first, as long as he gets at least one daughter."

"He'll be like you," Aled promised. "He just wants a healthy baby."

"He's getting a *big* baby," Suze complained. "I feel like a beached whale. This is shit."

"Should have put something on the end of it, then."

She blew a raspberry.

"Gabriel won't be able to come and visit for a while," Aled said. "He's a bit too fragile for the car just yet. But —"

"But you'll come," Suze said. "If Chris is there to look after Gabriel, you can come and visit us and take lots of pictures for them."

Aled hesitated. His gut clenched at the idea of Gabriel being so far out of reach, however temporarily.

"Um —"

"Of course you will," she said briskly. "He'll kick you out to make sure you do. I'll text him and make him promise."

"Bitch."

"You know it," she said cheerfully. "Anyway, he's got a little time. This monster is definitely going to be late. The midwife came to see the home birth arrangements yesterday and did a quick exam and she

69

doesn't think he's even in position yet. I'm drinking loads of raspberry tea to try and get everything moving, but so far, I'm just peeing a lot."

"Well, if you text Gabriel that he needs to throw me out, I'll text Tom something."

"What?"

"I read that the only proven way to bring on contractions is nipple stimulation."

"If it would get things going, I'd be up for that."

"Fine. Congratulations on his son."

Her voice dropped. "You wouldn't."

"Try me."

She scoffed. He held his ground. And after a couple more seconds, they both dissolved into childish sniggering.

"You *do* feel better," she said approvingly.

"Yeah."

"I'm glad Gabe's home and he's going to be okay. And I'll see you hopefully in a week or two to meet your nephew!"

"If the vertigo—"

"Honey. He'll be okay," she insisted. "It could have been much worse and it wasn't. You can handle anything else."

Aled chewed on the corner of his lip. For the first time since the accident, it felt like Suze was right. He'd nursed a fear of losing Gabriel for so long, the lack of pressure inside felt euphoric.

"I know," he murmured. "Now."

"Have a good day, sweetheart."

As he hung up and leaned back in his chair to go over the budget report, Aled finally felt as though the projections meant something, and he could keep his brain in the office instead of leaving it at home.

But he still watched the clock, waiting until he could leave again.

Chapter Eight

Chris was surprised at how quickly the three of them settled into a routine.

He got up early to go for his morning run and would get back in time to wave goodbye to Aled heading out to work. He'd shower then take the empty breakfast plates away from Gabriel and join him in bed for a few episodes of whatever garbage he was watching. Then he'd leave Gabriel for a midday nap and go downstairs to wash up, tidy or do his core training in the back garden if the sun was out and the neighbour's wife wasn't ogling from behind her ceanothus bushes. The afternoon usually saw more TV until Aled came home, then Chris would make dinner while they did... whatever they did, and the three of them would eat in the master bedroom like they were students living in a tiny studio flat with nowhere to put a table. Sometimes they spent the evening together playing cards or watching a film, and sometimes Chris would take refuge downstairs or go on another run.

He didn't move back into the spare room.

It was surprisingly easy to share space with Aled. It wasn't awkward or uncomfortable when they mutually ignored one another, and he didn't seem especially interested in Chris' life or presence. Some might have found it off-putting or offensive, but Chris had been shy since the day he was born, and appreciated the borderline apathy. If Aled wasn't interested in conversation, then Chris couldn't feel pressured into having one. And if Aled was happy to ignore him, then Chris was content to be ignored.

And thankfully, Gabriel was too tired to push the issue just yet.

For the first four or five days, he stayed almost exclusively in bed, Chris only being really required to help him get to the bathroom and have a shower each morning. And much as Chris wasn't a fan of sex or nudity, the shower hugs were kind of nice. Gabriel effectively just held on to him in a prolonged hug and passively let Chris scrub him down each morning. And Chris learned that if he did it after breakfast, it would knock Gabriel out for a nap far more effectively than the drugs that the doctor had sent them home with.

There was only one downside.

Chris' cock didn't agree with the rest of him about how revolting and unnecessary having sex was. Or about how grim it was to have a throbbing erection attached to his groin like some stray mystery meat at a dodgy kebab shop. Chris could barely tolerate the presence of his dick when it was just there for pissing and filling out his briefs. When he could feel his own pulse in it and it turned a horrific shade of purple that would be a sign of a major infection anywhere else on his body? No thank you.

And if Chris merely thought Gabriel was mildly pretty naked and covered in soap and water, his cock thought Gabriel was the sexiest thing it had ever seen.

And Chris *hated* it.

He hated getting hard. He hated jerking off. And he especially hated the wet, sticky, awkward social encounter that was sex.

But Gabriel wasn't up to their usual solution. Usually they would have a bland conversation while Gabriel rode his dick with as little movement and as tight a grip as possible, to keep Chris' mind off it but his libido far more satisfied than a simple hand job would allow. And Gabriel could barely sit up without the vertigo kicking in. So Chris tried to bottle it up, having an angry wank in the bathroom the first day it happened, and crying through another on the day after that.

But Gabriel had vertigo, not dementia.

"Hey," he said on the third day, as Chris helped him back into bed. "I know you're hard."

"It's difficult to miss," Chris admitted, feeling an ashamed heat rising in his face.

"M'just saying. I'm not wearing underwear."

Chris hesitated.

"Um. No. No thanks."

"Okay. But the rule still stands if you need to put it somewhere."

Chris denied it, left Gabriel for his nap, and stared at the bathroom ceiling while he took care of it himself later.

But—

The rule still stood.

If Gabriel didn't wear underwear to bed, Chris was allowed to fuck him in his sleep.

Gabriel liked being used, apparently. He often wanted sex without being bothered about having an orgasm himself, and he got a mental kick out of being fucked like an object rather than a person sometimes. Chris was barely aware of it. That was Kevin and Aled's business, not his.

Usually.

But Aled had issues with doing anything where Gabriel couldn't instantly retract his consent—like sex in his sleep. He wouldn't touch him if he wasn't fully conscious and aware, and apparently Kevin was hung so it wasn't possible to *stay* asleep. So early on in their relationship, Gabriel had asked Chris to screw him while he was out and see if that helped with Chris' own issues.

And...it did.

Creepy as it sounded, the lack of response helped. It still wasn't what Chris would call *enjoyable*, but it killed his libido for a good couple of weeks afterwards and it didn't make him want to crawl out of his own skin with disgust.

But jerking it in the bathroom did. Daily erections did. Cum on his own hand *definitely* did.

And he cracked on Thursday.

He'd taken a longer run than usual, hoping it would help, but it hadn't made the slightest bit of difference. His dick started stirring the moment Gabriel looped warm, wet arms around his neck, and it rested between their stomachs, hard as iron, by the time Chris had finished washing the still-too-short black hair hiding the surgical scars on Gabriel's scalp.

"I'm done," he said.

"Sure?"

"Shut it."

Gabriel smirked, but shut up. He sat on the closed toilet to carefully rub himself dry, resting his head against Chris' waist to have his hair combed. He could have sucked Chris off then and there, but a blowjob was the worst of all possible options, and he ignored the cock waving in front of his face like he couldn't even see it. The tug of grateful shame in Chris' gut hurt.

"Okay. Let's go."

Gabriel insisted on walking back to the bedroom — albeit putting so much of his weight on Chris and the walls that it was more for show than actual *walking* — then collapsed into the bed with a deep sigh.

"Want anything to wear?"

"No."

"Want the TV back on?"

"No. Sleep."

"Okay."

Gabriel burrowed into the pillows. Chris kissed the back of his head, then slung the towel over the radiator and retreated to the bathroom to take care of business.

And paused.

Gabriel had refused clothes.

So…no underwear.

He'd be out like a light in a matter of minutes. And masturbating wasn't working. Chris knew from experience that actual sex would put an end to the matter for a good few days. That was all he had to do. One fuck, then he could ignore his dick for maybe a week.

As opposed to seven days of jacking it.

He curled his fingers around the edge of the sink and stared down his reflection. Gabriel had given him permission. It would solve the problem for several days instead of several hours. Gabriel would even like it when he figured out it had happened. And Aled was at work, so it wasn't like he was going to walk in to find Chris fucking their unconscious boyfriend.

He took a deep breath and counted to ten.

Then opened the bathroom door and returned to the master bedroom.

Gabriel was already asleep, fingers twitching lightly on the pillow. He preferred sleeping on his front — apparently the vertigo was less impactive that way — and while his arms were coiled around the pillow, his legs were askew and slightly open. Chris gently nudged his knees farther apart and didn't get so much as a murmur. When he knelt on the mattress, the dip didn't seem to register.

Gabriel was under.

And Chris was still achingly hard.

He didn't mess around with foreplay. He liked cuddling and chaste kissing just fine, but even that was too much in a sexual situation. Instead, he almost clinically fingered Gabriel until he was loose and a little wet, then lay down over his back and slowly pushed his way inside.

And gritted his teeth against the shudder that rocked his spine.

Two parts revulsion, two parts arousal, it was a violent jerk from head to toe that finished the preparation. Gabriel mumbled as Chris bottomed out, and Chris waited for a long minute, just relaxing over Gabriel's body and breathing through the mixture of lust and self-loathing warring in his brain.

God, he hated this.

God, he *needed* this.

After weeks of nothing, Gabriel was even tighter than usual and it hurried things along. The almost too-hot warmth on the head of his cock and the resistance to his thrusts didn't let his sex drive drag things out. He didn't thrust *hard*, but hard enough to make a difference. And Gabriel lay asleep and unaware underneath him, as though Chris was just wanking into a warm body.

But it worked.

It was over quickly in a short, brutal orgasm that left him gasping for air. He pulled out in a hot, slippery rush. Cum followed. He'd have to change the bedsheets later.

And Gabriel simply mumbled something incoherent and curled his fingers into the pillows when Chris tucked the duvet back over him.

"Thanks," he whispered.

The afterglow burned on his brain as he took another shower, and his limp dick felt almost numb as he tucked himself into a pair of briefs. Satisfaction scrubbed out the shame. He wouldn't need to do it again for ages. The endorphins singing along his muscles were like the euphoria of finishing a marathon with a personal best. If Chris could only learn to *like* sex, he'd be as mad about it as Gabriel was.

But he'd tried that, and it had never worked.

The build-up and the act itself were always far worse than the aftermath. Chris hummed a happy tune as he washed the dishes and hung out some towels to dry on the line in the garden. He put out more birdseed and watched the tits fighting over it. By the time he heard canned laughter from upstairs, it was almost time for lunch, and he felt better than he had every morning since he'd arrived.

Gabriel was sitting up when he got upstairs and offered him a quizzical look.

"You fucked me?"

"Yeah."

"There's condoms in the bottom drawer if you want them."

Chris shrugged. "It was fine without."

"Okay." Gabriel switched off the TV and lifted his arms. "Bathroom. Then downstairs for lunch. I fancy a change of scenery."

It was a trap. Chris stooped to help him up, and Gabriel immediately locked his arms around his neck.

"Hey," he whispered, kissing Chris' ear. Chris stilled. "Did it help?"

"Yeah."

"Good." Gabriel squeezed. "I'm going to blame my wet dream on you, then."

Chris chuckled, and worked his arm under Gabriel's knees to pick him up.

"I can deal with that," he said.

The casual acceptance warmed him. The easy way he could just *be* around Gabriel relaxed him. They were polar sexual opposites, and yet Gabriel wanted to steal his cycling magazines over lunch and enjoyed a vegan bean stew that Chris had looked up online. With the ghost of sex gone, they cuddled on the sofa in a patch of sunlight streaming in through the conservatory doors, and Chris felt an entirely different kind of heat settling in his chest.

"Love you," he whispered.

Gabriel squeezed his wrist and kept talking about bicycle clips.

Chapter Nine

By Sunday morning, Gabriel was starting to feel cooped up.

Home was a thousand times better than hospital, but—a bedroom was a bedroom was a bedroom. He was getting bored of reruns and daytime TV. The midday nap was getting less necessary. And when he finally managed to say sitting up on the sofa all day without a single panic attack or collapse, he knew that he needed to get out and do something. Anything. Breathe some air that wasn't filtered through the smell of their own house. Feel some plants that weren't grown in pots. See unfamiliar faces. Stay relaxed and recovering, just...not in exactly the same spot.

The problem was Aled.

Chris was firm but not a natural worrier. He never had been, and he made a suitable nurse for it. If Gabriel wanted to fuck up his recovery, then that was on him as far as Chris was concerned. But Aled flapped and could be overly cautious. He always had been, and Gabriel landing himself in hospital hadn't helped matters. There was no way Aled was going to agree to going out somewhere without some significant guilt tripping.

Unless—

"What's your plans today?" Gabriel asked Chris over breakfast, which was finally being taken downstairs where it belonged.

"Depends. If Aled's staying home with you, might take the bike out and go for a ride. If not, I don't know. I'd like to take advantage of this good weather, though."

"Go for it," Gabriel said. "I'm going to try and persuade him to take me out somewhere. I need to escape the four walls for a little bit."

Chris snorted. "Good luck."

"I know." Gabriel eyed the ceiling. The bathroom was right above the kitchen, and he could hear Aled performing his usual trick of turning the entire place into a wetroom while he showered. "What do you reckon my odds are?"

"At about sea level."

"What if I talked him into sex?"

"Even lower odds," Chris said. "He's more likely to go and visit a brothel at the moment than do you."

"You did me."

"I don't like to hit you while I have sex with you."

"Technically," Gabriel said primly, "he very rarely hits me." He left off the reason why, being that it simply didn't turn Aled on much. Did plenty for Gabriel— except spanking, which just mystified him—but Aled wasn't so interested. He could be a little snobby like that. Violence wasn't as intellectually and sexually stimulating as a mindfuck, in Aled's lofty opinion.

Gabriel didn't entirely agree, but the mindfuck was amazing so he let it slide.

"Good luck, anyway," Chris said as he poured out his cereal. "And don't tell me about it if you manage to pull a miracle and get him to sleep with you."

Gabriel pondered it as he listened to Aled getting dressed overhead. He'd been more cheerful and relaxed since getting back to work — which was a first — but he was still…fussy. A point proven when he came into the kitchen in time to whisk Gabriel's empty plate away and stop him leaning over to slide it back onto the counter.

"Want anything else?"

"Nope."

"Everything okay?"

"Yep." Gabriel turned his head up for the kiss. "I was thinking we could spend some time together today. Go on a proper cheesy date or something. Chris is going cycling because he's a rude prick who wants to mock my inability to go places."

Chris didn't even take his eyes off his muesli to respond.

"Uh-huh," Aled drawled. "This wouldn't be you getting cabin fever, would it?"

"Nope," Gabriel semi-lied. "It's me wanting to spend some proper time with my partner."

To his enormous surprise, it worked. Aled made up some porridge with honey in thoughtful silence, then leaned up against the counter to eat it and nodded.

"We could go out for lunch," he said. "Have ourselves a little date."

They hadn't really gone on dates in years. To be honest, they'd never made a habit of it, even when they'd got together. They'd met thanks to Grindr, so their relationship had been about sex long before it had been about love. Usually, Gabriel only got taken on a date if it was going to lead to something kinky later.

So the d-word had his ears pricking up.

"A date sounds nice," he said carefully. "Italian? We could go to that nice place in town."

The nice place in town where he'd been forced to suck Aled off under the table on their very first visit.

"You're not walking up there," Aled said flatly.

"But their cannelloni starter is the *best*," Gabriel objected.

"I don't care if it's got a Michelin star. You're not walking all the way into town."

Gabriel pulled out the big guns. "I won't. You can push me in the chair."

The hospital had loaned them a lightweight wheelchair to help facilitate getting Gabriel home. As far as he knew, it had been folded away in the shed and forgotten about until he was due to go back for his follow-ups. He'd refused to be literally pushed around — he wasn't *that* ill — but the way Aled stopped with the spoon halfway to his mouth said his instinct was right.

"Look," Gabriel said. "I'm *bored*. I just want to get out of the house for a little bit and have you all to myself. And a cheesy lunch date at a nice Italian restaurant sounds perfect. But I get that you're worried about me falling, and I certainly don't want to end up back in hospital, so…I'll let you push me. We can park in one of the car parks in town and I'll stay in the chair."

Aled narrowed his eyes. "You promise to stay in the fucking chair."

"Yes."

"If you so much as *try* getting out of it, I'll not take you out until you can cartwheel on your own."

Gabriel hadn't been able to do a cartwheel before the accident and now just rolled his eyes.

"Deal," he said anyway.

And Aled said yes.

Well, technically he said, "Fine."

But that was a yes, and Gabriel could have cheered.

* * * *

The wheelchair wasn't actually that bad.

The vertigo was bad, but not so violent as the nausea in the car, and Aled surprisingly didn't freak out or go overboard when Gabriel had to wait and just sit there for a little while by the car after the fifteen-minute drive into town. Once the nausea had subsided, the bumpy ride of the chair down the uneven pavement wasn't too bad. As long as Gabriel kept his eyes on the sky.

But, God, it felt good to be out.

Gabriel was a natural extrovert, and he didn't need to *know* people to get a hit off them. He didn't need detailed conversations or crowds of friends. Just the simple act of saying hello to the waiter who put down a little ramp at the door lifted his spirits. Talking recommendations with the bartender for a good virgin cocktail made him feel better. Waving at a little kid curiously staring at two men having lunch together brought the smile to his face more easily.

"Thanks," he said once they'd ordered and been left in peace. "I needed this."

"I can tell," Aled said. "To be honest, so do I."

"Yeah?"

"Mm. It's easy to keep thinking of you as an invalid when you're housebound. And you're not. I know you're doing a lot better and you're going to be fine. But...I could use the reminder."

"Thanks for not being worse."

Aled chuckled. "Well, thanks for meeting me halfway. So why is this just us?"

"Sorry?"

"I thought you were trying to get me and Chris to date each other?"

"Well, 'date.'" Gabriel pulled a face. "I know you don't fancy each other."

"He's all right. I'd do him. But no, I don't fancy him."

"He'd not let you do him."

"Yeah, I know."

"And I do want you to get along and having you both around is *great* and long term I want us to talk about maybe keeping it this way permanently, but—" Gabriel nudged Aled's foot with his own under the table. "I kind of wanted a proper date, too."

Aled raised his eyebrows. "And what usually happens after one of our dates?"

"Yeah, little bit of that too."

"Ambitious."

"Hopeful. And optimistic. And up to it."

"Uh-huh. Keep working on the sales pitch," Aled advised dryly.

He had a single glass of red wine before switching to the virgin cocktails as well, and Gabriel both appreciated the teetotal solidarity—Gabriel was a recovering alcoholic, and next to never physically saw Aled drinking alcohol as part of their joint efforts to ensure he *stayed* recovering—and the glimmer of relaxation around the edges. Aled wasn't one hundred percent on guard. He wasn't the neurotic boyfriend who'd been at his bedside during Gabriel's hospital stay.

He was *Aled* again.

And that more than anything had Gabriel wanting an end to the dry spell.

"You want Chris to stay permanently?" Aled asked as their food appeared.

"Maybe," Gabriel admitted. "Having you both around all the time is great."

"Hmm."

Gabriel's stomach dropped.

"Is that a bad hmm?" he asked.

"It's a neutral hmm," Aled said. "I'm not sure how I feel about him living with us permanently. But...around in general? Yeah. It's nice having him around."

"I'll take that," Gabriel said quickly. "I mean, that house isn't really made for three, either."

They'd upgraded a little with the move, but more in terms of a bigger kitchen and a loft conversion to build a proper playroom for their sex games. They'd sacrificed the large living room in the old house for a larger back garden and proximity to the lake at the new one. It still wasn't fit for three fully-grown adults. Their neighbours had two teenagers, and Gabriel couldn't imagine squeezing *four* people into the place.

"True," Aled said. "Plus, we've been preoccupied with you. I like him fine, but this isn't exactly a good gauge of how we'd handle each other on a usual day-to-day basis, you know?"

"Yeah."

"We'll see," Aled said.

Gabriel loved him for the laid-back response. If Aled was overcautious and not much of a risk taker, he was conversely casual about Gabriel's lifestyle. He'd taken Gabriel's flighty nature when it came to relationships well in stride and had only interfered the once — and over a man who'd turned out to be very bad news. His typical approach was to just sit back and let Gabriel do his thing, and Gabriel adored him for it.

"Love you," Gabriel whispered, mindful of the setting but needing to let it out.

Aled raised his eyebrows. "You too."

"Just had to say it."

"Okay." Aled's foot rubbed his calf under the tablecloth, a mute gesture of affection that warmed Gabriel's heart. "Speaking of Chris, he mentioned that you're, uh, back at it?"

Gabriel snorted with laughter. "It?"

Aled rolled his eyes. "You know exactly what I mean."

"I do, but I want to know what he *said*."

"He stammered a lot and I think he said 'doing it' like a thirteen-year-old kid."

Gabriel grinned. "Oh my God. Bless him. Yes. We're 'doing it.'"

"Is that what you want after this?"

"Yes," Gabriel admitted. "But I'd like to spin this out a little before we go home, too."

"Dessert it is."

Aled's lack of objection was intriguing. Gabriel couldn't tell if it was the public space keeping him quiet, or whether he really was up for 'doing it' later. He hoped the latter. And something kinky and coercive and *bad*, in that deliciously good kind of way.

But he relaxed back in the chair and enjoyed his cannelloni, too. Enjoyed the French couple two tables over chattering about someone called Marc. Enjoyed the smells of a dozen different Italian meals sizzling away in the kitchen. Even enjoyed the barman's terrible singing along to an Adele song on the playlist. And he *really* enjoyed the homemade ice cream melting on his tongue while Aled muttered darkly about an Italian restaurant serving distinctly Cornish ice cream.

"Just shut up and eat it," Gabriel murmured, then closed his eyes as he added another mouthful of heaven to his palate.

Aled called him a drama queen, but Gabriel didn't care. He had a lunch date with great ice cream and later, he might get called a cock-hungry whore and have fresh cum fingered out of him. It was the first time he'd felt normal in over two months, even if he couldn't ride in a car without wanting to throw up, and even if he had to compromise with sitting in a wheelchair to get his date at all.

For the first time, Gabriel really felt like things were going to be all right.

Then the bill came, and all right turned into *better*.

"I've got it," Aled said, flashing his credit card at the waiter.

Gabriel paused, spoon still in his mouth.

In their whole relationship, there had never been such a thing as Aled *just* paying for dinner. In the beginning, it had been a lead-in to a game—Aled paid for dinner, so Gabriel owed him something, right? Fair was fair. Why would Gabriel accept Aled paying the bill if he wasn't going to put out later, huh?

Then after he'd lost his job and moved in with Aled to keep a roof over his head, it had been too scary. Too much like abuse creeping in around the edges. He'd not been able to switch off his paranoia and enjoy it for the playing it really was, so it had become one of their forbidden things. They'd religiously split the bill for months, and on the odd occasion it hadn't been possible, Aled had expressly said what Gabriel would pay for in return. Usually the next tank of petrol, given how much Aled burned through in his fancy cars.

But the game had crept back into their lives over the last few months before the accident, as Gabriel had shelved his paranoia and remembered how much he'd enjoyed. He loved a good coercion game, and while Kevin did outright violence best, Aled was a master at the mindfuck. And they'd often bled into secondary slavery play, where Aled wasn't satisfied by a coerced screw in the back seat of his car or a blowjob on the side of the road and would take Gabriel home to tie him to the bed and fuck him *properly*.

Gabriel's dick throbbed at the thought.

It had been too long. And the only trouble with Chris using him was that it gave Gabriel a really strong urge to fuck. *Brutally* fuck. He'd been used like a whore, and now he wanted Aled to hammer the point home. Literally.

Under the table, Gabriel slid his foot between Aled's.

"I forgot my wallet," he blurted out. "I'm so sorry. I'll pay you back."

Aled raised his eyebrows. He turned the card over in his hand, rubbing the silver letters of his surname. Gabriel bit his lip with his best nervous-but-seductive expression.

"All right," he said, and placed the card down on top of the bill. "I guess you owe me."

The bolt of arousal was intense, and Gabriel's hands shook as he unwrapped his after-dinner mint.

He was really, *really* fucked.

Chapter Ten

Aled woke up hard.

He wasn't all that surprised. Gabriel finally being well enough to go out, and his dropped hints at dinner, had sunk in. Aled had refused to take advantage last night, given how tired Gabriel was, but the morning was another story.

And, even better, Chris had already snuck out for his run.

Gabriel, sprawled in the bed beside him, was limp and deeply asleep, so Aled left him to it, slipping out to the bathroom and showering in near-scalding water, scrubbing his skin clean so it would feel even better when he dirtied and damaged it again with their game. He wasn't up for anything extremely violent, or even especially rough, but Gabriel would often scratch and bite if he was being supposedly forced.

Aled's dick twitched as he washed, and he bit his lip. Fuck. He shouldn't—Gabriel was recently out of hospital, and still suffering from vertigo. Sex, faux-forced or otherwise, had to be a bad idea.

But Gabriel had agreed when he'd paid for dinner. If he wasn't ill, Aled would have no qualms about stalking back in there and fucking him senseless with a hand over his mouth to stop him screaming before going to work. And by paying, he'd promised. He'd *promised*. If he didn't go ahead and play, how would Gabriel take it? At best, he'd be hacked off. At worst—

At worst, could he even think that Aled was turned off by the surgery scars?

His dick twitched again, seemingly determined, and Aled made up his mind. This wasn't any different from any of their other games. He'd done far worse than fuck him in bed. And if he could trust Gabriel to safeword, then he could trust him to tell Aled when he was hurting him.

And if he didn't safeword…

Aled dried off leisurely, then flushed the unused toilet, knowing the noise always made Gabriel wake up, even if only for a moment. He stalked out of the bathroom, all swagger, and sauntered back into their bedroom, drying his hair with the towel and unashamedly naked.

Sure enough, dark eyes blinked at him from the messy bed, and Aled smirked.

"Morning, beautiful."

Gabriel's, "Morning," was slow and hesitant, and Aled dropped the towel on the end of the bed, tugging at the sheets until they slid down to Gabriel's hips.

"I should be going," he said, "but you owe me one from last night."

Gabriel's fingers caught at the duvet. "I—I'll—when you get back?"

"What, and your bit on the side is here to stop me? Don't think so."

"But—"

"I paid for dinner. So you owe me. You trying to get out of it?"

"I—no. No."

"Because if you are, that's not very fair, is it? And I believe in fair."

"I'll pay you back. I—I'll go to the ATM today. I promise."

"Mm, it's not really the *money* I'm after," Aled persisted, pulling harder. The duvet came free, revealing that long, naked body, and Aled skipped his gaze over the withered leg and up to his chest. Rising and falling and getting faster.

"You need to go," Gabriel said weakly.

Aled laughed, crawling onto the mattress and clasping both ankles loosely in his hands. Gabriel tugged a little, but Aled didn't let go. "I can stick around for a bit longer."

"I don't—I don't want to."

"Don't play that game with me," Aled scolded, kissing Gabriel's knee and crawling over him, dropping his weight over Gabriel's good leg and clasping his head between both hands, Gabriel's arms tangled between them. "You enjoy it. You flirted with me all the way through dinner like you were going to come then and there, didn't you?"

"It wasn't flirting."

"You were making eyes at me like you were going to crawl under the table and suck my dick for dessert," Aled persisted, biting at Gabriel's ear and jaw. "You want this more than you need air. And you'll enjoy it if you stop sounding off."

Gabriel squirmed, wriggling an arm free—and slapped him. It wasn't especially hard, but the sound was loud, and Aled caught his wrist when it rose for another try and squeezed it until Gabriel cried out.

Then, just as abruptly, he let go and climbed off the bed. He wanted to give Gabriel the rough play that he'd asked for with their dinner contract—but he wasn't ready to really fight for it yet. So—

"I do like working in an office," he said, rummaging through wardrobes as if at random, but quickly finding a tie. "Means I've always got what I need."

Gabriel lunged for his phone, but Aled was faster, knocking it aside and catching Gabriel's wrist again. In a flash, he had them both roughly bound to the headboard, and gripped Gabriel's chin in his hand again.

"Just stop fussing and relax," he crooned, rubbing his mouth up Gabriel's cheek, and biting at his lips when they refused to part for him. "You'll like it. Promise."

Gabriel whimpered, but Aled was done talking. He didn't want to drag this one out—get them up, get them off, and get them settled. He could draw out their second 'date' if Gabriel preferred then.

He licked his way down that bare, twisting torso, and settled between Gabriel's hips, keeping his hands on Gabriel's inner thighs but only bearing his weight down on the right leg. Gabriel was already wet and swollen, and his pleas hitched and dissolved into whines when Aled wrapped his lips around his length and sucked.

Hard.

Down here, with Gabriel tied and trapped, Aled focused on pure pleasure. He knew exactly where to lick, where to suck, where even to bite, and performed a neat, torturous circuit of them all, homing in on the exact sweet spots that would completely shatter Gabriel's token resistance and undo him.

He kept it slow, too. This was no hurried fumble, no brutal screw. This was idleness, a man with a plaything and nowhere else to be and, as he moved lower, Aled spread the fingers of one hand up over Gabriel's flat belly and began to knead at him like a contented cat.

Or like a warning—Gabriel tried to close his legs, and only once, as the brutal twist that Aled delivered with finger and thumb, hard and deep enough to leave a bruise, made him whimper and go very still for a very long moment.

"Stop," Aled murmured as he transferred his mouth from one thigh to the other, "*fussing.*"

Gabriel shuddered as he bit down, then Aled chased the sweetness and reduced all resistance to nothing, holding Gabriel's hips fast when they began to move, holding him down as the shivering began to increase and latching on to suck him through the sudden crash of his climax, pulling on burning flesh even as its nerves exploded.

"There," Aled crooned, crawling back over Gabriel's lower half to plant a wet kiss on his breastbone. "I told you you'd enjoy it."

"Please—please just go, let me go, just—"

"I enjoyed it too," Aled murmured, tracking his lips up Gabriel's ribs and slowly beginning to push. The head of his cock breached that wetness slowly, and he felt Gabriel bear down and resist. "That's the problem with you, beautiful." He pushed harder, forcing his way into the tight, slick heat, like warm, wet silk. "You're *too* beautiful. Watching you come undone— fuck, gets me going, and that's why things end up not fair. I've given you dinner *and* a climax for free now. So where does that leave me?"

He began to thrust, deep, ploughing thrusts that shook the bed and had Gabriel wrenching at the tie. Aled usually preferred the short, sharp method, but with Gabriel spread out and used below him, he pushed himself up on his arms and *fucked*, watching with rapt pleasure as the motion rippled up that lithe body, as the punishing rhythm forced him to simply accept it, as Aled's own drive for release simply took Gabriel as a thing to be used, something to fuck into and catch the mess, no more than a tissue –

When his muscles seized and his blood boiled, Aled grabbed for those narrow hips and pulled, hard enough that Gabriel let out a muted sob and Aled came, flooding the silk with heat, spilling onto the sheet when he finally pulled out and leaking around his fingers when he pushed two roughly in, and began to massage.

"It's just how I get," he panted, like he'd never paused to fuck in the first place. "Your freshly-fucked look is a turn-on and I can't help it. Don't worry, though," he added, beginning to rub at Gabriel's abused flesh with his other hand, cupping him between Aled's wrists. "We'll break even. Just let me get it up again, and we'll be done here."

"No," Gabriel whispered, his voice raw. "Please, stop it, just stop it, *please* –"

Aled sighed, shifting up the bed – one hand still buried in Gabriel's pliant body – and covered that red mouth with the other. "Ssh," he crooned, biting at Gabriel's neck and feeling him shiver. "It's better if you don't lie, you know. We both know you're lying."

Gabriel whined, straining against Aled's hands, but Aled wouldn't let go. It was exactly what they both needed. Coercion, force, the thrill of a threat for Gabriel—and gentle enough for Aled that the worst would be a pair of bruised wrists.

That hot body wriggling under his was like a drug, and it didn't take long before Aled was hard again. He taunted Gabriel, rubbing him off only to pinch him and deny the climax at the last second, until his own cock was ready to sink back into that tight, wet heat. Gabriel cried. Aled kissed the complaint away and began to fuck him for the second time.

This time, it wasn't a plundering. He barely moved at all. Just twitched his hips every so often to feel Gabriel's thighs shudder against him. Better was the wet heat that squeezed his cock. Better were the breathless whimpers against his mouth. Better was the breast that he massaged in one hand, and the sobs when he bit into that sensitive neck. Better was the shudder with every touch, every movement, every murmur.

His second orgasm was a lazy, understated pleasure. He lay idle for a few minutes after, kissing the bruises he'd left on Gabriel's neck, before reaching up to undo his hands.

"I better get to work. I look forward to our next date."

Gabriel closed his eyes when Aled pulled out, and turned his face away from the kiss. Aled forced it on him anyway, before smoothing his hair and whispering the game-over signal. The next kiss was relaxed and willing, then Gabriel motioned for the pillows to bracket his head and shoulders.

"You okay?"

"More'n okay," he murmured. "G'wan. Go to work. F'k me again when you get home."

Aled laughed, patting a naked hip before heading for the wardrobe.

"You going to go back to sleep?"

"Yeah. Maybe."

"I'll let Chris know so he doesn't worry."

"Thanks."

He had dozed off before Aled was dressed, and Aled kissed his hair before tugging the sheets over him and leaving him to nap in his nest.

For the first time in months, he set off for work in a good mood.

Chapter Eleven

"Okay," Chris said. "How do you want to do this?"

It was Tuesday. Gabriel had spent the whole day texting back and forth with Kevin, another of his partners, and had finally decided that he was going to have dinner at Kevin's house.

Only problem was, Kevin couldn't come and pick him up.

And Gabriel's vertigo had eased enough for carefully walking around the house, stairs and showers excepting...but that mercy hadn't extended to cars yet.

"I need to lie down," Gabriel said.

"Okay."

"Can I put my head in your lap?"

"Want a pillow bracket?"

"Yeah."

"Okay."

Aled, listening by the door, nodded and headed up the stairs. Chris plucked the car keys out of the bowl and opened the front door.

"Back or on your side?"

"Back."

Chris was more than a little jealous of Aled's car. He always had the latest Range Rover, and the machine gleaming on the drive couldn't have been more than four months old. The high ride was a huge help for getting wobbly people in and out, and easing Gabriel down onto the back seat wasn't as awkward as it would have been in a normal car.

"Hey," Chris whispered in Gabriel's ear, stroking the shell to distract him from the nausea. "Reckon Aled will let me drive this one day?"

"Nope."

"Not ever?"

"Not ever. He once beat my arse until it bled for just *sitting* on the paintwork."

Chris grumbled, shutting up when Aled arrived with the pillow.

"Okay, lift up."

Gabriel's throat bobbed as Chris slid into the seat, but he kept the vomit down. Chris fluffed the pillow on his lap, then eased Gabriel down until his head was dead centre and Chris could fold up the pillow edges to bracket his skull as though he were carrying a very fragile egg.

"Better?"

"Mm."

Wedging his right arm around the pillow to maintain the bracket between his hand and his belly, Chris reached out and laid his other hand on Gabriel's stomach, stroking the twitching muscles until they relaxed.

"There you go."

"Thanks."

"So you going to spend the night at Kevin's?"

"Probably not," Gabriel said, wincing as Aled got into the front seat.

"Do you mind asking him if you can?" Aled asked. "Thinking Chris and I might as well go on a date of our own. Tacos and beer are calling my name."

"Oh my God, I do not want to be in your bed once you've had tacos," Gabriel said. "Okay. I'll ask."

He closed his eyes again once Aled started the car, and Chris stroked his hair in perfectly timed passes until they reached the motorway junction and the road smoothed out again. He didn't enjoy seeing Gabriel suffering, but he had to admit that riding with Gabriel's head in his lap was kind of nice.

And it was taking his mind off Kevin.

Chris had never so much as seen a picture of Kevin. The only thing he knew was that if Aled was the dominant who played dangerous games, Kevin was a complete sadist. Gabriel had largely refused to go into detail, merely saying that Kevin was 'Aled's sex on steroids.' Aled was a coercive fuck. Kevin was outright violent.

Chris was nervous, to say the least.

He didn't know much about Kevin sexually, but he knew plenty in other areas. He was the only partner Gabriel had who could exert control outside of sex — if Gabriel dropped out of contact for more than twenty-four hours, Kevin would start sniffing around to find him. If Gabriel drank alcohol, Kevin would take him and — something would happen to fix it, that Gabriel again hadn't told Chris much about. Kevin had a wife and a bunch of small kids, but Gabriel was regarded as extended family. He lived with Aled, but there was always another door open to him.

In a way, Chris supposed that he had very little to be nervous about. Kevin seemed more inclined to interfere than Aled, and part of Chris thought that Kevin would have showed up and kneecapped him if he didn't measure up already. The other part simply pointed out that Bristol was a long way from Leeds, and now here he was, fully moved into Kevin's territory.

Gabriel wasn't the only one feeling queasy.

It turned out that Kevin didn't live too far away. In no time at all, Aled was pulling up in a small street of tidy houses with identical front doors, coasting to a stop outside one with a work van parked on the drive and a pink scooter abandoned on the front lawn. Chris heard boots crunching on gravel, then the door by Gabriel's feet opened, and Chris' heart stopped beating.

Kevin was *huge*.

A black bodybuilder grinned in at them, a gold tooth flashing from the middle of a face framed by long dreadlocks. He was well over six feet tall, and his shoulders seemed six feet wide too. He could have bench-pressed a bus. A hand the size of a shovel squeezed Gabriel's ankle, and it honestly looked absurd. He could have snapped Gabriel's shin clean in two if he just held on a little harder.

"You must be Chris," he boomed.

"Uh. Yeah."

"Nice to meet you, man."

The handshake nearly ripped his arm off, then Kevin patted Gabriel's knees.

"You up to a walk, or you need to be carried?"

"I can walk."

"No he can't," Chris said. "He was nearly sick twice."

"Fuck off," Gabriel snarled, but Kevin just chuckled. "I like you. He can keep you."

"Can keep who I fucking want," Gabriel groused, but allowed himself to be dragged along the seat to the door. He looped both arms around Kevin's neck, and Kevin simply backed out and straightened as if Gabriel weighed nothing more than a bag of flour, carrying him like a kid.

"Bring my pillow!" Gabriel hollered.

Chris let himself out when Aled did, figuring it'd be weirder to stay if they were all going inside. The house was warm and bright. Thick carpets and plain walls were livened up by the framed photos everywhere. A formal family photo showed Kevin posing with a pretty white woman and a hoard of small mixed-race children. He could smell baking and hear cartoons playing beyond a closed door. A baby was whining, probably ready to go into a full meltdown. But they followed Kevin into a cosy living room littered with toys, where Gabriel was laid out on a white leather sofa that, despite the mayhem, was inexplicably clean.

"Tea?" Kevin asked.

"We're going to get going," Aled said, stooping to kiss Gabriel's forehead. "Can he stay the night? We were thinking of tacos and tequila."

"Sure thing," Kevin said. "We can put him up in the spare room, and I can drop him home in the morning. Not working for once."

"Judith put her foot down?"

Kevin pulled a face. Chris presumed it meant yes.

"See you later," Aled said. "Call if you need anything."

Gabriel gave a thumbs up. Chris bent for his own quick kiss, then followed Aled back out of the door and to the car. He sagged into the front passenger seat and took a long, deep breath. The relief made him shake, and he slid his hands under his thighs to hold them still.

"What's that for?" Aled asked.

"I've never met Kevin before."

"Oh, he's harmless."

"Like hell he is."

Aled laughed. "Okay, fine, he could commit murder with one hand. But he's harmless as long as you treat Gabriel right."

"What happens if you don't?"

"He smashes you up," Aled said. "Between you and me and the fact the restraining order actually *worked* on Gabriel's stalker ex, I'm not totally convinced Kevin didn't just up and murder him."

Chris whistled. "Uh. Good to know."

"Don't worry about it. If you still have both legs unbroken, Kevin's cool with you. So. Tacos? Have a night off from your dumb diet?"

"If it's trash food you want, then at least extend to a curry."

"Deal. I know a good curry house."

"Okay. And no tequila."

"Beer?"

"Beer."

The curry house that Aled had in mind turned out to be a takeaway out on the outskirts of Wakefield town centre. Chris had a soft spot for rogan josh, and if they couldn't really agree on comedians, they could at least agree on the importance of poppadums to go with a dirty curry. One pit stop at Asda for a crate of cheap lager later, and they were on their way home.

Chris had taken Aled for a wine drinker and the type to insist on plates and cutlery, but was proven wrong.

They put their feet up on the coffee table, cartons in laps, and cracked open the first lagers to the theme tune of a late-night comedy show.

"So tell me," Aled said as the contestants were introduced. "You and Gabriel. You in love with him?"

Chris blinked. "Well, yeah."

"Is he your first poly boyfriend?"

"He's my first boyfriend at all."

"Really? What about girlfriends?"

"Nope. Never been interested. In girls, that is. Had a few…there were a few men I would have liked to date along the way, and a guy I was sort of with for a little while—though I wouldn't have called him my boyfriend—but…well, you try finding a boyfriend who'll understand that dick's disgusting."

"No thanks. *I* don't understand that. Dick's great."

Chris just flipped him off.

"So you're…what, gay without the sex?"

"I guess."

"Is there a word for that?"

"I don't know."

He'd never really looked into it too hard. He'd tried going online a few times after Gabriel had first suggested he was asexual, but it was a hot mess of confusing words. Chris had barely finished school. He didn't have the first clue what anyone was talking about with romantic orientations and three-foot-long words like autochorisexual or aromanticism. He had no idea what a lithromantic was supposed to be. The jumble of terms was scary, and felt like…well, like he was pretending. It felt horribly like he was faking it. He worked in a bike shop and couldn't spell bicycle. What right did he have to go around spouting Scrabble winners like autochorisexual?

"You ever think sometimes you're too dumb to be queer?" he blurted out.

"You what?"

"I tried looking it up. If there's like...gay aces. Or whatever. And it's—" He waved a hand vaguely. "There's so many terms and they're all massive and complicated and they have these weird definitions that I don't understand. Only there's whole forums of people like 'oh yeah, this is me, this is totally me.' And I don't even get what they're talking about. I feel too stupid, so...so I just avoid it and I try not to think about it."

Aled grunted. "I don't know. I missed out on the internet as a kid. I was in university before we got a home computer. I like men and women, so I'm bisexual. That's about as complicated as I ever got."

"Gabriel suggested I was asexual so I looked it up. And some stuff I found says it fits. But then it was all what *type* of asexual, and was I—I don't know. Greyromantic or sex-neutral or all this other stuff I didn't understand."

He'd felt stupid. He hadn't even dared ask questions. Chris might be thick, but he didn't feel like being yelled at by angry teenagers for not getting it.

"I wouldn't worry about it too much," Aled said. "I doubt Gabriel's got a degree in queer studies either."

"He knew about asexual."

"Probably just means he's banged someone who's asexual before," Aled said. "I wouldn't worry about what to call yourself. If you're happy in your relationship, then that's enough, isn't it?"

"I don't know," Chris admitted. "Sometimes I feel like I'm the only man like me in the world, and it's fucking lonely. I'd like to think there's other guys out there like this."

"Seven billion people, there's bound to be."

"Yeah. In theory."

He knew he was being maudlin, but he couldn't help it. He'd spent years wondering what the hell was wrong with him. Aled's casual attitude wasn't something that Chris could really relate to.

"Look at it this way," Aled said. "You're kind of uptight about whether your sex life is normal, but there's going to be people out there who are freaking out because they're in a poly relationship and isn't that just called cheating?"

It brought Chris up short.

"I mean, I know you were twitchy that I might not be as chill with it as you two are, but you never went, 'Well, better not get with this guy, he's just cheating on his boyfriend.'"

"Because...he's not."

"'Course he's not. But some people don't get that and wig out," Aled pointed out. "Like you thought I might."

"Huh."

He had a point. Chris had been worried that Aled wasn't as relaxed as Gabriel made him out to be, but he'd never turned it around and asked himself if *he* was okay with Gabriel having other boyfriends. Because why ask? He just was. It didn't make a difference to him.

"I kind of like it."

"Polyamory?"

"Yeah. I mean, for him. I'm not really interested in having more relationships. But I—I know he loves me too, and…come on. Can you really see Gabriel being happy with so little sex in his life?"

"Nope. When he got together with me, it was part of the deal. If I couldn't accept that he'd have other boyfriends, then I could take a hike."

"He never really *said* that to me, but he brought you up within minutes, so I knew there was someone. And I'm okay with it. I feel like some of the sex pressure is off, you know?"

Aled hummed.

"No?"

"It's probably different for you," Aled said. "He has different sex with me and Kevin—and the rest—so there's stuff he only comes to me for. Or only Kevin. Or whoever. But I guess if you're not into any sex at all, it'll be different. Though—" He shrugged. "I guess there's no pressure for me to choke him, given Kevin does it."

"Guess so." Chris sipped his beer and eyed Aled curiously. "Why do you like it?"

"Sex?"

"No, Gabriel being poly."

"I don't feel anything about it," Aled said. "It is what it is. He likes options. Long as I know he loves me, I'm not bothered."

"You never get jealous?"

"Nah. He's my world, and other people visit that world sometimes. No big deal. It's not for me—emotionally speaking, anyway—but it's how he is. Who am I to change that?"

Chris nodded. "I guess we have that in common, then."

"You a one-at-a-time type guy?"

"I think so."

Aled raised his can. Chris clanked them together.

"To keeping it simple," Aled said.

"To simple."

"Or as simple as Gabriel ever gets, anyway."

Chris snorted with laughter, but as he turned his attention back to his food, he started sifting through the conversation in his head.

Maybe Aled was right. Maybe it was time to stop worrying so much and start going with the flow.

And where better than here, in their home, where he had no other option?

Chapter Twelve

Gabriel's first hospital appointment was on Thursday, not a full week after he'd been released in the first place.

He stewed over breakfast and was silent as they set him up in the back seat with Chris' lap and pillow combination for his head again. The wheelchair was folded up and put in the boot. Aled drove with the radio off for the first time in maybe forever. And Gabriel knew his foul mood was infecting the others, but—

Fuck it, he damn well didn't care.

Gabriel *hated* doctors. Nurses. Hospitals. GPs. Pretty much any and all medical establishments were the devil as far as he was concerned. From the family doctor when he was thirteen—who had told him that he was confused then snitched on him to his mother so he'd spent the next few years being beaten for 'pretending' to be a boy—to the nurses on the wards who'd called him Gabby even after Aled had written his name and pronouns in large red letters on his whiteboard. Gabriel had never had a good or even neutral experience with doctors and had a special form of contempt for people who insisted they were caring souls or that ignorant medical staff were a thing of the past. Ignorant, overprivileged cunts. He'd blocked more than a few interested parties on Grindr who had turned out to be medical staff, and had never looked at their neighbour at the old house the same way again after seeing her in her paramedic uniform.

So being wheeled back through the main entrance wasn't exactly putting him in the best of moods.

Thankfully, Aled knew from experience to keep his mouth shut, and Chris had either been forewarned or could sense the danger. Neither tried to offer empty promises or weak condolences. In fact, they didn't speak. Chris pushed the chair, Aled carried the folder of drugs and paperwork they'd been given on discharge and the three of them arrived in grim silence outside the consultant's office. The sunny receptionist did nothing to improve Gabriel's mood. He sat and continued to stew for a full forty-five minutes until his name was called.

"You're coming with me," he said when Aled hesitated. "Both of you. I want witnesses."

"To what?" Chris asked.

"To my complaint when the cunt is out of line again."

Chris' teeth clicked as he shut his mouth.

The nurse that showed him into the office delayed the inevitable by taking another blood sample for infection screening and checking his vital signs. She chattered to Aled, who put in the effort to be friendly back, but Gabriel completely ignored her.

"Okay, honey, Dr Thompson won't be a moment!"

He clenched his jaw. *Honey.* She was only about twenty. There was no way she was going around calling the likes of Aled or Chris honey.

"Hey," Aled murmured, squeezing his shoulders. "Take it easy. You're not staying."

Gabriel nodded jerkily and tried to cling to the idea. He wasn't being re-admitted. He wasn't staying. He just had to suffer through this hour with the idiot, then he could go home again and it would be at least another week.

Shoes squeaked. The door swung open. Dr Thompson breezed in like a flagship returning to port without a scratch, but claiming to have won the war. He washed his hands in silence before turning to Gabriel and offering a thin smile…to Aled.

"We don't usually allow more than one chaperone into the exam room."

"Tough," Gabriel said.

"I'm afraid —"

"There's plenty of room. They're staying."

"It is hardly necess —"

"I don't trust the lot of you. It's very necessary. So we can carry on with both of them here, or I can leave."

He wanted Dr Thompson to tell them to leave. He wanted to go *home.* But of course, he only earned another curled lip before the doctor backed down.

"Very well. And how are we doing…Mr Lazarri?"

Gabriel heard the distinct pause before his title.

"Great," he ground out.

"How's the vertigo?"

"Better."

Finely plucked eyebrows rose a fraction. *"Better?"*

"Yeah. I can walk short distances and I haven't thrown up once."

He wasn't going to mention the panic attacks if anyone rolled over in bed. Or that the stairs were forbidden. Or the car was like a rollercoaster no matter how carefully Aled drove. Or the fact that he had to be held and washed in the shower like a little kid.

"Hmm." Dr Thompson snapped some gloves on and took Gabriel's head in his hands, tilting his face down and parting his hair to see the scar. Although they'd shaved most of his head, the scar itself was very thin and mostly obscured when he spiked his hair up. In another couple of weeks, it would vanish under the new growth entirely and Gabriel could forget about it. "The external wound is healing well. Are you taking the painkillers?"

"No."

"The anti-nausea aids?"

"One a day."

Dr Thompson stepped back, snapping off the gloves. "If you could just walk around the room a little for me."

Gabriel squeezed the arms of the chair before pushing himself up. Immediately, his stomach rolled. He locked his knees and straightened, willing himself not to sway or wobble. He wasn't about to give Dr Thompson the satisfaction of seeing him off his game.

One foot in the front of the other, Gabriel crossed the room. And felt as though he were climbing a mountain.

But he did it in a straight line. Sweat pooled in the small of his back as he returned to the chair, and he sat down a little too hard in it, but it had been a straight line to the window and back. Black spots danced at the edges of his vision, and the dipping pull of vertigo dragged on his senses, but he didn't wobble.

Aled's hands returned to his shoulders with a gentle squeeze, and Gabriel tried to relax his jaw.

"Hmm," said the doctor. "I see."

"You see?" Aled echoed.

"It's obviously very difficult for him."

"*He* is right here," Gabriel replied waspishly.

"Is that because of vertigo, muscle weakness or nausea?"

"Vertigo," Gabriel said. "But it's getting better."

"You must be prepared for the prospect that it will never completely go away."

Gabriel swallowed thickly. It wasn't so much the idea of having vertigo for the rest of his life as the flat, careless delivery.

"Fuck me, you don't even care," he muttered.

He was used to doctors viewing him as more of a curiosity than a patient. Most of them had never knowingly met a trans patient and were either absurdly fascinated, or low-key appalled. But the one thing he couldn't quite get used to was the way they divorced him from his own humanity. He wasn't a patient to them — to Dr Thompson. He was a *thing*.

"I'm done," he said. "You can discharge me. When I need more anti-nausea drugs, I'll go to my GP. At least she doesn't talk over my head to my boyfriend."

"Discharging you would be against medical advice."

"That's your problem," Gabriel said. "I'm out."

Chris didn't move with the chair, so Gabriel stood up. Thankfully, his shoulder was caught and he was put back by one of Chris' firm hands before the brakes were released.

"Mr Lazarri —"

Gabriel shook his head. Chris pushed. Aled stayed behind — presumably to argue with the doctor a little — but when Chris paused in the mouth of the office,

Gabriel said, "Cafe," and the chair started forward once more.

He felt—

Strange.

Usually when confronted with a prick that obnoxious, Gabriel exploded. It had been a while—the last time he'd really blown up at someone, it had been a hookup leaving him money like he was some kind of prostitute, and that had been years ago—but he'd expected to end the appointment by shouting and maybe getting thrown out.

He didn't know what he felt about just walking—sort of—away.

"Do you think I did the right thing?" he asked as Chris pushed him into the lifts.

"No."

"I couldn't just— He's such a fucking— I—"

Chris rubbed his arm. "I get it."

"You don't."

"I get it. I don't really understand why he gets to you that much, but I get needing to walk out on someone who does."

"Ever done it to a doctor?"

"Haven't seen a doctor in years, so…"

Gabriel coughed a laugh. "I wish."

"For what it's worth, I don't think it's necessarily critical," Chris said. "You're home. You *are* getting better. If your GP can prescribe your medication then…"

He trailed off as the lift spat them out on the ground floor. Gabriel watched the volunteers directing visitors as Chris parked him up by the coffee shop in the front of the lobby and went to get something. When he came back, Aled was at his heels, carrying a cardboard bucket of sweet tea.

"You all right?" he asked, drawing up a chair to sit at Gabriel's left.

"I guess. Sorry."

"It's all right. He was being a knob."

Gabriel pushed the tea away, an unpleasant heat rising in his face.

"M'gonna cry," he whispered.

"C'mere, then."

It made it better and worse all at the same time. He wasn't angry. He was *tired*. Tired and depressed and so fed up, so done, that Aled's calm words and gentle embrace broke the dam. Gabriel burst into tears, and the shame was worse than the cold anger upstairs. He didn't want to do this anymore. He didn't want to be in hospitals, talking to doctors, taking drugs.

"I can't do this," he whispered.

Sharp, jagged edges of pain crowded around his skin and needled him. He'd take a lifetime of vertigo. He'd take the daft measures to ride in the car. He could live with those. He could manage.

But he couldn't manage this anymore.

"I want to go home. And I'm not coming back. Not unless I collapse and I need an ambulance. I'm not doing this anymore."

No more scans, no more sneering doctors, no more Miss and Gabby and false smiles over the top of his head at his partner like he'd had his brains scooped out while they pulled the depression fracture back out and drained the bleed. No more memories of his mother screaming in his face, of the family doctor who'd scoffed at his coming out, of hookups in nightclub toilets because it was safer than going home with strangers who hadn't figured it out yet.

No more any of it.

He wanted to be *him* again. With Aled and Chris and Kevin. His family. Who saw him for *him*, and not for anything else.

"Take me *home*."

Aled squeezed. Chris kissed the back of his head.

"Okay."

Chapter Thirteen

"Go for a run," Aled advised once he'd stacked the lunch plates by the sink. "I'm going to get the kit out and make Gabriel feel a little better."

Chris raised his hands. "And you can stop right there. I'll do the dishes then go down to the shop for more fruit."

Aled gave him a thumbs up, and headed back up the stairs. He wasn't actually going to have sex with Gabriel, but let Chris believe what he liked. It would still involve Gabriel getting naked, and that was probably borderline for Chris already.

E4 was playing on the telly when Aled walked into the bedroom, some sitcom with canned laughter trying to lighten the mood, but Gabriel was staring out of the window. It was starting to rain. The view was nothing but a grey murk.

"Hey." Aled squeezed a foot under the covers. "You okay?"

"Mm."

"Want me to call Kevin?"

Gabriel shook his head, sliding down into the pillows.

"Just feel —" He waved a hand. "I don't know. Flat. Empty. Adrift."

Aled rubbed his shin. "Want me to anchor you?"

Gabriel shrugged a little, so Aled shifted up the bed and leaned in to kiss his cheek.

"Tell you what," he said. "Let's get you in a tight wrap and lock in all the pieces, hm?"

It wasn't a game, as such. It wasn't even really all that kinky. Aled had come up with the idea after reading an article in the news about vests for some anxious or even autistic children that mimicked a tight embrace and helped calm them down or keep them level. Given how Gabriel could be a little wobbly if he safeworded a scene gone wrong, they'd decided to try out the wrap to see if it could help.

And so far, it had worked like a charm to bring him down out of the panic or the misplaced fear.

But those had only been for scary safewords. The odd time they'd experimented with a brand-new thing or pushed a boundary and it hadn't gone well. The knife. The branding iron. The one and only time Gabriel had permitted him to try bloodplay. Aled had never tried it for...well, depression. Gabriel wasn't a particularly morose person. Until this spell in hospital, Aled had seen him sad or miserable or upset, but never in a prolonged, emotionless, almost apathetic manner.

He'd never seen him *depressed* before the accident.

"Okay."

Aled kissed his forehead, then got up and headed for the wardrobe. The master bedroom had built-in wardrobes, and a small suitcase sat in the bottom of one, half-hidden by Aled's suits hung up ready for the working week. It was so unassuming that any visitor would have assumed it was just somewhere to put a cabin bag for holidays.

But Aled opened it to find their toys.

They had a *lot* of toys, between his collection and Gabriel's. Neither had much interest in dressing up, but Aled had an extensive collection of bondage gear, and Gabriel had both dildos to be fucked with, and strap-ons to fuck somebody else, although Aled was never on the receiving end of one of those. Their gear was split into two halves in the case—one for external use, the other for internal—and Aled ignored the plastic bag of internal toys in favour of the neatly rolled length of silk and the heavy bag of leather straps.

"You okay with naked?"

"Yeah. But imagine the boxers."

Gabriel's boxers were a silent red card to any funny business, and Aled cracked a smile.

"Sex isn't on the cards right now, beautiful," he said as he closed the case. He shut the wardrobe and placed his equipment on the side table, jerking open one of the drawers to retrieve a bottle of massage oil. "Come on, then. Let's get you stripped down."

Gabriel was only wearing his underwear and pyjama bottoms, and Aled slid his long limbs out of the cotton with practised ease. Gabriel simply relaxed and let him, placid as a doll. The silk was a dressmaker's roll, long and wide, and Aled laid a length down like a bedsheet before laying Gabriel out on top of it, face down and naked. A few drops of massage oil were placed along the nubs of his spine, then Aled rested his full weight between Gabriel's shoulders and raked his palms down.

The groan could have rattled the rafters.

Aled worked in silence. The knots of weeks without proper exercise or decent posture were savage. The stress was even worse. Gabriel moaned like a porn star under his hands for almost half an hour before his back resembled something like a spine again, and he lay quietly and simply breathed as Aled massaged the back of his neck and put paid to the tense lines around his eyes. He didn't bother with anything below the waist. Not only was it too likely to give Gabriel the wrong idea in his current messy state, but Aled didn't need the temptation. So he worked from the waist up, dissolving every last flicker of resistance, until Gabriel had melted into the sheets and silk and resembled a human being again, instead of a miserable patient.

He was almost asleep before the warmed towel came into play.

"Ssh," Aled murmured when he jumped at the first pass of cotton. "Just relax."

The towel blotted away the remains of the oil, and Aled ducked out to rinse and dry his hands before returning and unrolling silk strips from his pile. The bottom sheet was to get Gabriel's skin used to the soft sensation, but the strips were the real McCoy.

Aled worked from the feet up, encasing both feet individually in silk before wrapping his legs so they were bound together. Firm, but not tight enough to leave marks on the skin. The first leather strap was locked just above the ankles, and two more either side of his knees. By the time Aled reached Gabriel's waist, he could not have moved his lower half if he'd been paid to do it.

And he showed no inclination to do so.

Every inch of him was relaxed. He only stirred when Aled slid the chest harness under his lax body, and even then it was simply to shift until his breasts were tucked into the right position. Silk covered the harness, then Aled rolled him over to lock his arms over his chest with more leather and another layer of silk, before turning him gently back over and rolling his head to the side on a pillow.

Bound.

Tight, but not painful. Unyielding, but not in itself hard. The idea was an embrace, and Gabriel relaxed within the confines of the fabric in much the same way he relaxed into a cuddle. Quite literally gathered together and strapped into place, the effect was psychologically similar. All the pieces pulled back together and secured safely in a warm layer of softness.

"There you go," he whispered. "Fan?"

"Please."

He turned on the fan that sat atop the dresser, turning it until Gabriel's hair waved gently, then picked up the final pieces of the jigsaw. Blindfold. Gag.

Usually for sex, Aled used a ball gag because Gabriel found it humiliating and therefore hot. But the leather strip was gentler on the jaw and allowed for more comfort. Gabriel sighed deeply when Aled tied it, and his eyelashes fluttered once before the blindfold obscured them.

Then Aled stripped and climbed into bed.

He tucked Gabriel up against his side, laying that dark head on his shoulder and curling his arms around lax shoulders. Trussed, gagged and blinded, Gabriel would be surrounded by *Aled*. He would be wrapped in a warm security and held by a trusted presence. All he would be able to sense was Aled's smell, Aled's heat and Aled's heart thumping away near his ear.

And sure enough, he sagged in Aled's hold and relaxed.

His heart slowed. His breathing dropped. He didn't quite sleep—there was an edge of too much awareness—but Aled dozed with the warm cocoon in his arms and felt the day leech away from Gabriel's body.

There was little Aled could do about doctors and dysphoria. Nothing much he could say to defend Gabriel from the world. No remedy for what went on inside Gabriel's head. And for the most part, someone as confident as Gabriel didn't need to be rescued. For the most part, he could fight his own battles and Aled watched from the sidelines, holding his coat and cheering him on.

But not *every* time.

And in those exceptions, he could provide this instead. Counteract a little of it with love. Lock him down in a secure shield and hold him until his brain had righted itself. If Gabriel needed to go to Kevin's later and have the day strangled out of him, then Aled would drop him off. If he needed to be chained to the bed like a breathing sex toy and used, then Aled would do it. And if he needed to be adored—rare, but it did happen—then Aled would gladly worship him.

But for now, he needed to be *held*. So Aled would hold him.

For as long as it took.

Chapter Fourteen

Summer was turning out to be a long, dry and hot one.

And Chris didn't like any of those things.

Rain helped cool him off on a long ride. Spring and autumn in the country were more enjoyable than bland summer greenery, especially when it came to colour and clear views. And heat was just...*urgh*.

But there was a plus side — it meant the hammock in the garden was always available, and they had quickly discovered that rather than fuelling vertigo, the hammock surprisingly helped. It had a lot of excess cloth to cocoon its occupants in security, and the gentle swaying seemed to translate to comfortable and secure even through Gabriel's head injury. Weirdly, the one thing that should have made the vertigo downright dangerous was the one thing that could lay it to rest.

So even if the midday snooze was a thing of the past, Chris more often than not found himself lying in the hammock, Gabriel's weight spread out over him from chest to foot, and one of Chris' legs draped artfully over the side to prod the garden wall every now and then to keep them rocking. Sometimes they lay in silence. Sometimes Chris would read aloud from one of his magazines, or — if Gabriel was having a good day and the hammock hug wouldn't be needed for very long — they would simply talk.

Rarely did the plans overlap, so Chris was more than a little surprised when Gabriel interrupted a review of a new route being tested out on the Irish coast with, "How long are you going to stay?"

Chris paused, then closed the magazine and dropped it onto the grass. He knew a long conversation when he heard one starting.

"However long you need me," he said.

"And what happens if — when I don't?"

"When," Chris agreed gently, then shrugged. "Then I go home, I guess."

Gabriel hummed.

"What?"

"What if I don't want you to go home?"

Chris snorted, even as he silently agreed with the sentiment. "I have to go home eventually."

"Why?"

"Aled's not going to pay me to be your boyfriend."

"That's about a job. That's not about going home. We have jobs here."

Ah.

Chris hesitated, unsure of how to put his thoughts into words without causing offense. Gabriel had lived all over and didn't seem to feel attached to physical places very often. But Aled had lived in the same corner of Yorkshire all his life and seemed disinclined to move, and Chris —

"I'm not so keen on the north."

"Why not?"

Chris sighed. "I don't know. I feel out of place. People are different up here."

"How?"

"I don't know," he repeated. "They just...are. The slang's different, they talk different. If someone strikes up a conversation at a bus stop, you're not about to get shanked..."

Gabriel laughed. "Oh come on. You live in *Bristol*, not London."

"You still don't talk to strange men at bus stops."

"Okay, okay..."

"It's uncomfortable," Chris said finally. "Here — right here — is great. Being with you. Even with Aled. But outside the front door...I don't know. It doesn't fit right."

He knew exactly where this was going. And he didn't quite know where he sat on the issue.

"You want me to stay?"

And Gabriel nodded.

Chris blew out his cheeks. On the one hand, he wanted to stay with them. Getting to see Gabriel every day instead of sending constant text messages and snatching moments here and there when one or both of them had time off work, as if they lived in different countries, was getting old. He'd gone from shy and ready for the relationship to dissolve at a moment's notice to actively missing him and planning a future in his head. He'd almost accidentally found a partner, and he'd been woefully unprepared for the impact on his plans and lifestyle. For the first time, leaving was going to be harder than staying.

But staying *here*?

The north wasn't home. Chris had been born and bred in North Somerset, and anything north of Birmingham was a foreign country to him. Gabriel had a mixed accent, tempered by a London upbringing, but Aled's could be impenetrable when he got going. They ate their food wrong. The houses were built funny. Chris had given up trying to figure out what he was supposed to call a roll. And maybe it was just a Wakefield thing, but who the hell was designing the road layout in West Yorkshire anyway?

The strangest thing was that Chris didn't even know what he was holding on to back home. He didn't particularly have friends in the area. He'd quit his job without thinking twice. He and Mum skirted around each other with mutual wariness, and he'd never had a father. His brother was gone. Nailsea itself was boring, and although the cycling scene in Somerset was brilliant, it wasn't the best in the country by any means.

But something felt —

Off.

The hardest part of the army hadn't been the endless boredom in Germany, the bullying, or even losing people. It had been the sense of being *lost*. The feeling that he was in a place he wasn't supposed to be, and the itching need to go home all the time. It was losing Tim that had finally made Chris give it up, but the urge to go home had been there from the day he'd caught the train and left in the first place.

And it was here, too. Under his skin, scratching away. He needed to go home. He needed to go *back*.

"Here's the thing," he said. "I miss you when you go home after a visit. More than I ever expected. I don't like being so far apart all the time. And I — yeah, okay, I've been thinking about whether this arrangement can play out long term. I'm not sold on living with Aled all the time, to be honest, but living with you? Getting to see you every day instead of stealing time and calling in sick so I can get a few more hours before your train home? It's been great. And when you're better, it's going to be almost impossible to walk away from that. It's going to *hurt*."

"There's a but," Gabriel whispered.

"Yeah."

"Yorkshire's the but."

"Well, I mean, the north in general. Yorkshire's nice enough. But it's—I feel—I shouldn't be here. There's this constant pull to go home. This is a nice holiday, but...but that's what it is. It's almost like this isn't real life and, eventually, I have to go back."

"Don't let Aled hear you underselling God's own country like that."

Chris cracked a smile. Gabriel tapped his chest, then hummed.

"What?"

"Just thinking," Gabriel said. "Don't tell Aled I said anything, okay?"

"Uh, okay."

"I think eventually we're going to pack up and move south."

That was news.

"What? Really? When?"

Chris hadn't picked up on that at all, and he almost sat up before remembering the stupid nature of doing that in a hammock. As it was, he physically twitched. Moving? They were considering *moving*? Aled seemed bound to West Yorkshire, and Gabriel sure as shit wasn't going anywhere without him. Chris had never entertained the idea of them coming down to *him*.

"I don't know," Gabriel said. "He's not said anything about it or dropped any hints, but he's been...lonely since Suze left. He calls her almost every day, he's almost quit the gym now she's not there with him, and he doesn't really go out anymore. She and Tom were his social circle, really, and he's not bothered to make a new one."

"Lots of married guys—well, okay, you're not *married*, but same difference. My point is, loads of married guys don't go out much."

"Yeah, but I think he misses it," Gabriel said.

"Has he said that?"

"Of course not. Their nights out involved getting shitfaced, and we don't talk about the A-word."

"Ahh."

"But I expect one day he's going to decide he wants to live down there nearer to them," Gabriel said.

"And you'll go with him?"

"Of course I will."

"So potentially..."

"I mean, that's *Cornwall*, not Bristol, but I don't know where Aled's supposed to find a marketing executive's job in Cornwall, so maybe we won't go all the way south. Maybe we can stop sort of...Bristol-ish."

"Bristol-ish," Chris echoed.

"And I'm like you, I can just find a job whenever," Gabriel said. "So—what then? What if that happened?"

"That changes things," Chris admitted.

Having them down south? Closer, if not right there. He wasn't going to bank on Bristol—Cornwall was still a fair distance from there, if Aled's goal was to be near his friends—but Exeter was a possibility. It lay close to both, though Chris didn't have the faintest idea about whether Aled's kind of work was found there. Chris wasn't even sure what a marketing executive *did*.

But what if they went to Cornwall itself? What *about* Cornwall? He'd been to Cornwall plenty—it was the summer holiday destination as a kid, and Falmouth had been one of his brother's favourite places, so it had even been a refuge and a place to mourn once he'd gone. It wasn't home like Somerset, but it wasn't another planet like Yorkshire. It was—familiar. Not quite home, but not quite alien either.

"If we came south, would you stay?"

"Yes."

Gabriel slid an arm around his ribs and squeezed. Chris squeezed back, pondering it. He wanted this. He wanted hammock cuddles in the summer and to relocate to the sofa in the winter. Gabriel didn't really game with him much, but he'd shout encouragement or slag off the other players while Chris did his thing. He wanted to gang up on Aled to persuade him into trying cycling, but to be able to go on his runs alone without Gabriel trying to talk him into shortcuts every five minutes. He wanted to have the room to be antisocial, because there'd always be someone else around to take the pressure off. He wanted his own space, but for the open door to be feet away instead of hundreds of miles.

He wanted—

He wanted *them* to be home, as well as the south.

"Don't tell Aled," Gabriel repeated. "He's not said anything yet and he needs to figure things out for himself or he gets really tangled up and dithers forever. But I think now Tom and Suze are starting a family, it won't be long."

Chris nodded, stroking his nails gently up Gabriel's arm.

"We've got a while yet," he said. "You can't even do stairs yet, so I'm hardly going to be packing my bags next week."

Gabriel grumbled.

"Chill out," Chris said, kissing his hair. "You're getting better. You couldn't even get to the loo on your own when you came home. Or have sex. You're getting there."

"Who says I'm having sex? Having a nap while you fuck me doesn't count."

"Aled texts me when I shouldn't come in the bedroom," Chris said dryly.

"Oh."

"Yeah. Oh."

"Well, at least you get a warning."

"Thank God. I don't want to see your boyfriend's arse…"

Gabriel laughed. "It's a nice arse!"

"Says you. It's fat and white and *ginger*."

"Ginger? Try again. The carpet hasn't matched the curtains for a while now…"

"Oh, *gross*—"

They bickered a little, then Gabriel settled back down and Chris resumed stroking his arm. The contentment was making him drowsy. Or maybe that was the sun.

"You're getting better," he said. "But I'm not going anywhere just yet."

And despite his anti-north convictions, maybe the pull of the south and home weren't strong enough to drag him free anymore.

Maybe.

Chapter Fifteen

Chris was right, though.

He *was* getting better.

When he'd been in hospital, the vertigo had been so severe that he could barely open his eyes when lying flat on his back, but here he was, propped up on the pillows on Kevin's sofa, a bowl of Judith's special — and sinful — carbonara in his lap, and watching a Disney movie with the girls. He'd never been into Disney, or kids, but even Gabriel thought it was quite cute when Grace tried to sing along with Jeremy Irons.

Just like being in his own house was being at home, so was being in Kevin and Judith's. Judith — Kevin's wife and his main submissive — was a warm and welcoming presence, and like an aunt even though she was only a few years older than Gabriel. Kevin would beat him senseless in the workshop, roleplay the most violent rape and torture scenarios imaginable with him, then text him selfies with the girls on days out, pick him up from work if it was raining, have him round for dinner just to check in that everything was okay. He'd finally succeeded in ditching the alcohol because of Kevin and Judith. Hell, he was probably *alive* because of Kevin and Judith. And so it was that Gabriel felt perfectly at peace on their sofa, Lily sitting between his feet as though he was an extension of the chair, with a man who'd given him literal scars crawling around on the floor with Grace pretending to be a hyena and his heavily pregnant wife breastfeeding their youngest in the armchair.

"Did you pick a name in the end?" Gabriel asked. Judith had miscarried their very first baby — Rose, whose tiny handprints had been cast in plaster and were still on proud display on the mantelpiece, six years after her loss — and so they had a tradition of not naming the babies until they'd passed the seventh month. It had been coming up when Gabriel had been put in the hospital. Now, she couldn't be more than two weeks from her due date.

"Well, we were thinking Leah, but this little lady is far too active for a Leah. She's going to be a boxer like her daddy."

Kevin fist-pumped the air, and Gabriel laughed.

"Definitely a girl, then?"

"Oh, they couldn't work it out from the scans, but I know," Judith said loftily.

"You can't know," Kevin said. "It's a boy. Kevin Junior."

"Have I been wrong before? No. Shut your mouth."

Gabriel grinned. Judith was a sub like he was a sub. All right, so they were a little more lifestyle than Gabriel liked for himself — if Aled tried to control his money or tell him what to wear every day, there would be serious problems — but Judith ruled the roost. Kevin might be the one in charge in the bedroom, but he was completely controlled by her in every other aspect.

In any case, the kids didn't have a clue. They were too young to understand BDSM or polyamory yet. Gabriel was just Dad's friend from work. The garden shed was just full of boring old junk. Dad sometimes worked evenings as well as during the day. They had no idea, and Kevin intended on keeping it that way for as long as possible. Gabriel supposed it made sense. It would be too easy to teach them they needed a man to slap them around if they got the wrong idea about how it all worked.

Although watching Grace dragging her father around by the hair, he wondered if kink wasn't genetic.

"So if she's not Leah, who is she?" he asked.

"Zoe. Still has a lovely sound, but a much more active sort of girl," Judith said.

Only three names were outright banned, as far as Gabriel knew. One was Rose, for the simple fact that they couldn't forget their firstborn and didn't want to try. The second was his deadname, although it had a double protection in that Judith thought it was a hideous name anyway. And the third was Victoria, Judith's racist sister who refused to acknowledge her nieces' existence due to their black father.

"Lily, Grace, Gabrielle and Zoe," he said. "That's nice. You need a boy soon, though."

"He'll be a boy," Kevin said. "Lily, Grace, Gabrielle and Kevin Junior."

"We are *not* having a Kevin Junior!"

"You might already have a boy," Gabriel said, gesturing at Gabby. "You never know. She might take after me."

"Are you Gabby's daddy?" Lily asked.

Gabriel cracked up laughing. Kevin groaned.

"No, honey."

"But she's white like you."

"She's white like Mummy," Gabriel said. "Nothing to do with me, darling."

"Why?"

"You know how you need a piece from Mummy and a piece from Daddy to make a baby?"

"Yeah…"

"Well, they have to be different pieces. Like you need a knife and a fork for dinner. Doesn't work with two forks or two knives. And Mummy and me have the same pieces, so we couldn't make a baby."

"Oh," she said. "But why's Gabby so white?"

"She's only little," Gabriel said. "You were very white when you were a baby. And she's got those lovely dark eyes like you and Daddy, doesn't she?"

"I guess…"

"And I think that's bedtime for the pair of you," Kevin said loudly, scooping Grace up off the carpet and blowing a raspberry on her belly. "Come on. Bath time."

"I'll take them," Judith said, buttoning herself up. "This little madam needs another wash too. Come on, you two. First one to the bath gets to pick which bubbles!"

Talk about where babies come from was immediately forgotten, as was Jeremy Irons. They tore off upstairs, and Kevin rose from the floor to help Judith out of her chair and start tidying up the mess. He took Gabriel's plate as well and swiped a path through the toys back from the kitchen. Gabriel reached for the remote, abandoning *The Lion King* in favour of some *La*

Liga game. He didn't keep up with football much, but it made for nice background noise.

Then the bathroom door closed.

"We've got ten minutes," he said.

"Ten minutes to w — hey!"

Kevin's fists yanked on Gabriel's T-shirt, hauling him up. The room spun. He was dropped face-down over the arm of the sofa like a rag doll and clung to the cushions in dizzy shock for a moment as his jogging bottoms and briefs were yanked down his legs.

"No!"

A hand pressed into the back of his neck, shoving his face into the seat. The sudden shift from laughing friend and father of three to dangerous potential rapist was as dizzying as the head injury, and a thrill shot through Gabriel's blood even as he fought. He burned hot within seconds, and Kevin's hard grip did nothing to quench the flash of arousal.

"Shut up."

"P-please, you can't — "

His hair was yanked, and the corner of the cushion shoved between his teeth.

"I said shut up, you fucking whore."

The insult went straight to his dick. So did Kevin's fingers. They rubbed him in hard, punishing strokes that had Gabriel grinding against the sofa in seconds.

"Knew you wanted it."

Metal clinked. Denim scraped the backs of his legs. A leaking head dragged from his dick to his arse, then back in to settle against his cunt. Firm fingers gripped his neck again.

"Keep your cunt open and your mouth shut."

Gabriel squeezed his eyes shut as the enormous head breached him. It was like being fisted. Dry. It *hurt,* and he whimpered as his lower lips closed around the shaft. No pauses. No time to adjust. Just inch after inch after inch of a dick the size of a forearm, scraping and dragging and *forcing* its way into him—

Balls touched his leg.

Above him, Kevin groaned. Straightened. His dick shifted and Gabriel shuddered violently. He could come if Kevin fucked him right. Rub himself off on the cushions. Just—

Kevin curled his fingers into Gabriel's hips and drew back.

"*Quiet*," he hissed.

Then thrust.

Hard.

His dick *punched*. Gabriel howled. Thankfully in time with a cheer from the football match on the TV. He gasped raggedly as the pressure eased again, then choked on empty lungs when the next thrust came too soon. Too hard. He couldn't catch his breath, never mind come. Kevin wasn't fucking him—he was *hammering* him.

Gabriel worked the cushion out of his mouth with shaking hands and curled his fists into it instead. His dick was on fire. His cunt shook. He wanted to come, but he was afraid to clench. He wanted to be beaten so there'd be something else to think about except the fuck. He wanted—he wanted—

The dick tore out of him. He was dragged by the neck, down off the sofa and onto the rug. On his back. A hand clamped around his mouth. A dick forced its way back into his abused pussy and began to pound once more. An immense weight bore down on him, pinning him down, and a wet tongue bathed his ear until he blinked away tears of revulsion.

"Look at yourself."

Gabriel looked down.

At the hips smashing into his own. At his stomach rippling with every punch. At the gleaming cock sawing him in half. At his tits wobbling between their chests. At his swollen dick, begging to be touched.

"This is what you're for, you little cunt."

Gabriel moaned.

"You're for fucking. You're built for cock. So when I say you're to open your legs, you do it. You don't fucking argue. Got it?"

Gabriel nodded frantically. The hand vanished. The tongue in his ear slithered into his mouth and he choked on the filthy kiss as the fucking sped up. Fuck, it hurt. He couldn't breathe. Couldn't think. Couldn't move to take more of it or ease the pain. He could only lie there and be fucked, be violated, be r —

The thought burst. He shoved a hand between them. The edge of his nail grazed his dick.

"Fuck!"

The floor buckled. Kevin's body slid over his own. The vertigo yawned like an empty abyss — and Gabriel blinked, the climax fading, and he was held by the jaw, finger and thumb digging bruises into his skin.

He was empty.

Not wet. Not leaking cum onto the carpet.

Empty.

And a long, hard, wet cock was lying on his stomach.

"Did I tell you that you could come?"

"N-no, sir," he whispered.

"Where do you think this is going now?"

"No-no-no, please — "

The hand. Silenced. The tipping room. Rug under his stomach. Air on his arse.

He cried.

Sobbed like a child into Kevin's hand as his arse was split on that truncheon of a cock. Lay there shaking in silent agony as it sank deeper and deeper into him. Listened to the football from a thousand miles away and was jerked back into the present when hot cum stung at his torn backside.

"Be grateful we don't have more time," came the dark warning.

His jogging bottoms were yanked back up his legs, but his underwear wasn't returned. He clung to Kevin's arms as he was lifted back onto the sofa and whimpered when he was buried under an incredible weight and a hand pushed up under his shirt to toy with his nipple.

"Please...no more..."

"We're done when I say we're done, slut."

Fingers pinched. His nipple ached. Gabriel gasped and it was stolen by another dirty kiss. When he tried to pull his head away, it was wrenched back and his tongue bitten.

"What did I just say?"

"I'm—I'm sorry—"

The bathroom door opened. Someone squealed.

"Daddy, Daddy, come and read me a bedtime story!"

"Coming!" Kevin yelled and got up off the sofa. Gabriel gasped at the sudden abandonment, brain and body both reeling. Kevin groped his crotch hard, then let go with a low laugh. "We'll finish this later."

"But—"

"It's happening whether you like it or not, so I suggest you think of ways to be nicer to me so I don't just shove up it your arse again."

"*Daddy!*"

"Choose."

He stomped off upstairs, leaving Gabriel staring stupidly at the ceiling. His arousal warred with his vertigo, creating a slightly scary disorientation. He'd always been helpless when Kevin fucked him—that was part of the attraction—but it had never felt quite so absolute before. It had never felt quite so *dangerous* before.

He jacked off again, fucking himself on wet fingers, as the family moved around upstairs. The second climax rattled a few brain cells back into place, then he wobbled to his feet and clung to the furniture to get into the kitchen and wash his hands. Cum was dribbling down the back of his legs, but he couldn't do much about it. And no doubt Kevin would punish him if he tried.

Getting back to the sofa took an age, and he switched the football off to doze on the cushions. Judith was pacing the landing with Gabby, crooning a lullaby. Kevin was doing silly voices in the girls' room. Gabriel had time. He could just close his eyes for a moment, right?

"Hey."

A hand squeezed his elbow. Gabriel blinked the grit out of his eyes, and Kevin flashed a wide grin.

"Evening, Sleeping Beauty."

"Urgh. Sorry. What time is it?"

"Nearly nine. Come on. I'll run you home."

"M'kay."

It took much more effort to get off the sofa the second time. His head spun. Knees buckled. Kevin's chuckle was low and warm in his ear, and large hands cupped his waist. Gabriel clung for a moment before trying again and was gradually supported out to the car.

"Back seat," he whispered.

"Okay. Need a cushion?"

"Yes, please."

He had to wait in the front while Kevin removed the baby seat, but soon he was laid out across the back, head cupped in a soft pillow and the centre seatbelt knotted around his waist like a harness. He closed his eyes to avoid the shuddering ceiling as Kevin started the car, and drifted to the music. It was all getting easier. He *was* getting better. It was just—slow. Frustratingly slow.

The engine died, and he blinked against sleep again as Kevin opened the door by his feet—and climbed in. He snapped the door shut again and crawled up over Gabriel's body, his massive frame shrinking the space until Gabriel felt like he was being buried alive.

"What—"

"Earlier was a little rushed."

Thumbs hooked into Gabriel's jogging bottoms and yanked them down.

"And you were putting up a fight. You going to do that again?"

Gabriel arched with a deep groan of pleasure as his abused cunt was stretched once more around a hard dick. His left leg was pinned to the seat back, the right shoved out until his calf hooked around the headrest. Kevin's weight hurt. His teeth on Gabriel's nipple, straight through his T-shirt, hurt more.

"N-no, sir."

"That's more like it. Let's have a little enthusiasm this time."

"Fuck," Gabriel whispered as Kevin shoved his T-shirt up and began to play with his tits. "Oh fuck. Fuck-fuck-fuck—"

"Fuck what?"

"Me. Fuck me, sir. Please. Harder. *God*, yes, just like that—"

"See? All it takes is a hot cock and you're moaning like a bitch in heat."

"*Fuck* yes."

He never got it vanilla off Kevin. There was always an edge. Some kind of pain. Some humiliation.

And it came in the form of blood.

Kevin's teeth were buried in his breast, and the cock inside him sawed in such long, slow, almost lazy thrusts that sex clearly wasn't the point. And when the pressure around his nipple grew too much, and tears came to Gabriel's eyes, he realised what was going to happen.

"Please don't. *Please*. It hurts—"

"Like a little pain's ever stopped a slut like you."

Gabriel gulped for air as he felt the first beads of blood bubbling up through the skin. He didn't like bloodplay. It was scary. Too real. Too much.

And he could safeword, he supposed, but there was a better way to stop it.

As Kevin's teeth bit down and the blood began to run down Gabriel's side and pool against his trapped arm, he rocked his hips up into every thrust. He didn't really have a G-spot inside, but he had a large clit that served just as well as a dick. And in the tight space, it

142

didn't take too much until Kevin's washboard abs grazed it with every thrust.

"Oh fuck," Gabriel whispered as the blood make Kevin's teeth slip on his skin. "Harder. Please, God, fuck me harder. Break me open. Make your cum run down to my knees. *Harder—*"

Kevin's control slipped. The next thrust rattled Gabriel's teeth in his skull. Hands tightened against his ribs.

"Fuck yes, just like that, show me what a fucking whore I am—"

He could moan like a porn star if that was what would get Kevin to come faster. He could get himself off on dick if he needed. Around the blur of pain and the sick, slick feeling of hot blood, the electricity was building. A storm was churning. There would be lightning strikes, and—

"*Fuck!*"

Thunder.

Kevin's moan rumbled like a breaking storm on a distant horizon. The flood of hot cum in Gabriel's stretched pussy washed away the sick sensation of the blood on his tits. The messy kiss tasted of copper, and Gabriel opened his mouth and let Kevin's tongue violate him.

Because when he pulled out—

Gabriel came on the hot, slippery rush, his own orgasm so intense that he squirted. Kevin laughed darkly in his ear and wiped it off with his hand. Gabriel was forced to lick it clean, tasting sex and spunk on heated skin, before his legs were tucked back together and his throbbing, oversensitive dick pinched between finger and thumb.

"What are you, then?"

"Your whore, sir."

"Damn straight. You going to tell me no again?"

"No, sir."

"Good. Let's get you home to your boyfriend, then. Maybe he'll want to put his own mark on the other tit."

Gabriel tugged his top down as Kevin got out. The fabric was ruined in a matter of minutes. His breast throbbed in agony, both awful and delicious. He tried to ignore the colour.

Kevin had just pulled over on the side of the road to fuck him, so it was another fifteen minutes home. By then, the pulse of pain was echoing in time with his vertigo, and Gabriel had to be carried to the door. Aled simply raised his eyebrows at the state of him, and he was carried straight up to the master bedroom, the sheets turned down and the TV paused on some sitcom or other. Chris was nowhere to be seen. Maybe that was for the best.

"Look after yourself."

Kevin's fingers hooked behind his ear, and the kiss — while still tasting of seedy sex in the street — was warm and soft. Gabriel curled his toes and tugged on a stray dreadlock as Kevin pulled away.

"Thank you."

"Welcome, sweetheart. See you soon."

He passed Aled in the hall, who simply rolled his eyes and offered the first aid kit.

"Yes, please."

"Chris has gone to bed," Aled remarked. "We didn't think we'd be getting you back tonight."

"They're taking the kids to the beach tomorrow," Gabriel said. He wriggled out of his top and tried to relax as Aled wiped down the bites with antiseptic gel and baby wipes. It stung like crazy, and he winced.

"Uh-huh. What did you do to deserve this?"

"Put up a fight."

"Should know better than that."

"Mm. Hey!"

His legs were pushed open. A baby wipe scraped the mess from his thighs and groin, then a dry finger probed his loose hole.

"What? I'm not good enough for you after him?"

"No! It'll just—it'll hurt."

Aled flicked the plaster over his damaged nipple. "That hurt. You weren't complaining."

"I was!"

"You let him fuck you anyway." The finger slid out. The bed rocked. Then Aled's hard cock slid in, and Gabriel grimaced at the burn. "Look at me."

He opened his eyes, and yelped when Aled's hand sealed his mouth shut and those fierce eyes hovered just inches from his own.

"Remember who you belong to?"

Gabriel nodded as Aled began to leisurely thrust. His cunt gaped. The wet sound was humiliating, and his face burned as Aled chuckled darkly above him.

"Yeah, that sounds like you hated it. Let's get you nice and tight again."

Gabriel screwed up his face and clenched when Aled slipped the nipple ring out and began to suck on his other tit. Oh fuck. *Fuck*, this was going to hurt.

But of course, they knew him. They both did. Knew exactly how and when and why to hurt him. It hurt like hell—and he came before Aled was even close to finishing.

And after that, he lay drifting in a post-orgasmic haze, the pain prickling the very outsides of his awareness, as his blood stained the sheets and oozed in thick, wet stripes over his abused chest.

Right where he wanted to be.

Chapter Sixteen

It was eleven o'clock before Aled's phone lit up on the table.

"Gabriel's up," he said, but heaved himself to his feet. "I'll go."

Chris just grunted, still trying to scrape a clod of dogshit off his shoe. His morning run hadn't gone too well.

Aled climbed the stairs to a surprising quiet and found Gabriel still sprawled out on the bed, topless and littered in bites and bruises. His abused tits were a little puffy, but when Aled touched them with the palm of his hand, he wasn't decked or sworn at. Though a single eye opened and regarded him with cold superiority.

"This is *your* fault," Gabriel said.

"You came back fucked-out and horny," Aled countered. "How about a shower?"

"Yes, please."

"Okay. Up you get."

He was fairly steady on his feet, so Aled didn't get into the shower with him, instead sitting on the closed toilet to keep an eye on him. He rummaged through the first-aid kit while he waited, and once Gabriel stepped out into a warm towel, Aled made him sit on the counter and took care of the bites.

"Kevin really did a number on you, huh?"

"Yup."

"Not like you to let either of us get away with bloodplay."

Gabriel shrugged. "Don't get used to it. Hurts like a bitch."

"Fair enough," Aled said. He stuck the last plaster into place and kissed the soft flutter of skin by Gabriel's breastbone, disturbed by the calm beating of his heart. "Feeling better after being used and abused, though?"

"Yeah. Feel more normal."

Aled pulled a face. "Only you would consider having your breasts ripped up normal."

"Yeah, well, you enjoyed it too."

"I did." He kissed the soft spot under Gabriel's ear. "I suppose there's a positive side to this dependency."

"What's that?"

He stepped back and folded his arms over his chest. "What are you going to give me not to just put you back in bed and lock the door?"

Gabriel laughed, but looped his arms around Aled's neck and nuzzled his cheek.

"Red," he said. "I'm too hungry for playing games right now. Maybe after breakfast."

"Okay. Breakfast in bed. Eggs on toast?"

"Poached. Please."

After the heat of the shower, Gabriel was much shakier on his feet than before, but Aled got him back to bed without too much trouble and left him to find a TV channel that he liked. By the time he returned with freshly poached eggs on whole-wheat toast—all the white bread had mysteriously vanished since Chris had moved in—Gabriel was sprawled out in the middle of the bed, wearing absolutely nothing, and watching some Gordon Ramsay reruns.

"Stay with me," he said, patting the sheets. "Is Chris on his run?"

"It's nearly lunchtime."

"It's never!"

"It is," Aled said. "He trod in some dog crap, so he's swearing to himself in the kitchen trying to clean his shoes. It's a bit intimidating."

"What, Chris?"

"Yeah."

"He's a pansy."

"He's got a penknife to the soles of those things and I fear for my balls," Aled said flatly.

"Whatever."

"Want me to go and film it?"

"If he's that scary, you wouldn't dare."

Aled pulled a face but conceded the point. He stole the remote back to find something decent on the telly and settled in to play with Gabriel's hair and watch their feet tangled up together at the bottom of the bed. If anything gave Gabriel's gender history away when he was fully clothed, it was his feet. Small. Delicate. Dainty arches. He'd look stunning in a pair of heels, but Aled knew far better than to ask for it. Gabriel would probably murder him with the desired stiletto just for suggesting it. So Aled kept the fantasy to himself but couldn't help stroking those pale feet with his own, watching them squirm and wiggle away only to return once he'd stopped for a few minutes.

Aled was in the mood for more.

But not the coercion or the abuse of last night. He was in the mood to explore. To hold Gabriel down and worship him for once. It usually had to be done as orgasm denial to keep Gabriel interested, but Aled felt like something sweet. Something long, uninterrupted, and appreciative.

He fumbled his phone out of his pocket and sent a text.

Me: Don't come upstairs

Chris: Gross

Me: ;)

"Done?"

"Yeah."

He took the empty plate—then put it out on the landing and closed the bedroom door. Gabriel watched through narrowed eyes as Aled opened the wardrobe and removed some ties, and folded his arms under his naked breasts as Aled dropped them on the end of the bed.

"I got fucked three times last night by some *very* abusive men," he said. "You expect me to open my legs again?"

"Yep. Hands on the headboard."

"But—"

"Hands. On. The headboard."

Gabriel hesitated, then said, "The minute I feel a twinge, you're getting safeworded." But curiosity always killed the cat, and he put his hands up to the headboard. Aled tied each wrist to a bedpost, leaving Gabriel flat on his back and stretched out too much to even bend his elbows. Then he did the same to his ankles, leaving Gabriel spread-eagled and barely even able to arch his back. Aled kissed his inner thigh before getting off the bed. He nipped into the bathroom for the razor and a bowl of warm water. On his way back, he paused to rummage through the dresser at the foot of the bed. He hadn't played with the edible lube in months, but there was still a generous bottle of mango at the bottom of the sex drawer, and he added it to his collection.

"Okay," Aled said, kneeling between Gabriel's knees and arranging the items on the sheets. "This is what we're going to play. I'm going to shave you. And when you're polished up, I'm going to use this whole bottle of lube. And you're going to enjoy the hell out of it."

He actually preferred Gabriel with some hair, but Gabriel thought it got in the way of the best orgasms and tended to shave. Every now and then he'd pay Judith to wax him properly, but he didn't feel safe going to salons for it. But he'd not been able to shave himself for weeks, much less get waxed, so his bush was wild, the way Aled liked it, rather than tidy or non-existent like Gabriel preferred. Sure enough, he groaned appreciatively when Aled wet the razor.

"Fuck, I love you."

"I know."

"And that's it?" he asked as Aled gently nudged the razor between his thigh and his labia and began to smooth the wiry hair away. "Just shave me and eat me out?"

"That's it."

Gabriel dropped his head back to the pillow and closed his eyes.

"I *suppose* I can let you do that."

Aled chuckled. "Why, thank you." He bent his head to kiss Gabriel's bellybutton, then sat back and carried on.

Much as he wasn't a fan of the bald look, there was something soothing and almost erotic about shaving the hair away. He moved with a gentle, steady hand. The rough sound of the razor made a sharp contrast to the warm flannel wiping away clumps of black curls. The dangerous scrape of a blade so close to Gabriel's most sensitive areas was soothed by the cooling cream that Aled rubbed into every centimetre once it was bared. The clinical act of pulling each fold and crease smooth to catch every last hair was undermined by the breathy sighs above him and the slowly swelling dick nudging his fingernails. Gabriel's dick was nothing more than a clitoris engorged by years of testosterone therapy, but it was more sensitive than any cock Aled had ever wanked off, and he paused once he was done with the razor to dip his head and kiss the hood.

"Fuuuuck," Gabriel whispered.

"Want a blowjob to start you off?"

"Mm, yes please."

Aled set the used bowl and razor on the floor, then climbed back up and rested his elbows either side of Gabriel's hips, kissing the soft, warm skin of his abdomen just below the bellybutton. He was still lean from hospital food, and Aled gnawed lightly on prominent hip bones until the helpless giggles turned to protests, then moved lower.

When hard, the tip of Gabriel's dick could just about be held between Aled's lips. He pressed his tongue against it until Gabriel groaned, then massaged it with his mouth. It throbbed, echoing Gabriel's racing heart. The smell of the cream was quickly overcome by the smell of sex, and Aled paused for a moment to breathe it in before returning to the task at hand, and massaging Gabriel's dick with his lips.

Aled lived for the thrill, the edge, the violence, the psychological torture of their usual games. The cold rush of adrenalin and the sense of power. But there was something almost ethereal about this kind of control, too. Gabriel couldn't escape this if he tried. Aled could do anything he wanted, and Gabriel would be powerless to stop him. To have him like this, and yet do nothing but explore his body and draw him gently to ecstasy rather than drive him there by force—

It was wholly different kind of dominance.

Aled sucked him right through the climax. The ties groaned as Gabriel strained. The yell wasn't quite a word. But Aled didn't let go until the shaking had subsided and the breathless moans turned to whimpers, a protest against his mouth on oversensitive cock.

Aled drew off, kissed a jumping pulse on Gabriel's inner thigh and reached for the lube. He sat back on his heels, rolling the bottle between his palms to warm the contents, and conducted a quick visual examination, making sure Gabriel hadn't pulled the ties too tight around his limbs. Once satisfied, he twisted the cap off the bottle and squeezed his signature out along a jutting hip bone.

"Aled?"

"Mm?"

"No fisting."

"Wasn't going to, gorgeous."

"M'kay."

In fact, Aled intended on using his hands as little as possible. The mango lube was just the right mix of sweet and tart, and he smeared his signature out of existence with his tongue before nipping at the crease where leg met hip. He dipped lower to kiss warm, wet cunt — still relaxed from yesterday's brutal fuck and the gentle climax Aled had offered — before returning to the shaved-smooth labia and beginning to coat them in the sweet, slippery scent of mango. To avoid temptation, he slid his hands under Gabriel's arse and kneaded at his cheeks while he worked.

"Jesus..."

Mouth busy, Aled didn't deign to answer. He mapped both outer and inner labia, giving Gabriel's cock time to recover, before returning to it and coaxing it back to fullness. When that first mouthful of lube was spent, he trickled a cool stream straight down the length of Gabriel's dick and sucked it off in time to the shivers that racked his trapped frame.

"Fuck," Gabriel whispered. "Bite me."

"What?"

"I need to come. *Bite* me!"

Aled chuckled. He sank his teeth into Gabriel's thigh in a savage, bruising bite, and tightened his jaw when the headboard banged against the wall. Something wet and warm splashed against his cheek. When he let go, he laughed to realise Gabriel had come so hard he'd ruined the sheets.

"Better?"

"Mm." A knee twitched. "Want m'legs."

"Why?"

"Want to wrap my thighs around your head f'r the next one…"

Aled considered it as he stroked more lube around the shivering edges of Gabriel's cunt with his tongue. Being strangled by Gabriel's knees didn't sound fun. But slinging them over his shoulders and tongue-fucking him sounded much better.

"No," he decided, and blew on Gabriel's dick when he protested. "Another time."

He did yield to the temptation to eat him out, though. Burying his nose against Gabriel's cock to get as deep as possible, Aled mapped that familiar place with his tongue rather than his fingers or his cock. Short laps opened him up and deep probes had him moaning like a professional porn star.

One squeeze was all it took.

Aled ate the climax that struck Gabriel like a freight train, and pulled out only when it was over, to wipe his tongue on a heaving belly and kiss a thundering heart.

"You — you done?" Gabriel whispered.

"Nope. Still a good inch of lube left in the bottom of this bottle," Aled said and crawled up far enough to kiss his cheek. "How d'you feel about being turned over and your arse getting some attention for a change?"

Gabriel strained his head up. Aled granted the demanded kiss. It tasted of fake mangoes, sex and desperation.

"If you don't fuck my arse with your mouth *just* like that," Gabriel whispered against his lips, "then you're not getting lucky again for a month."

Aled chuckled. He didn't usually go for rimming, but there was a flash of furious demand in Gabriel's eyes that dared him to even try and back out of his offer.

And who would want to try and get out of that?

"Okay," he said. "Over you go. And if you keep quiet, I'll suck your dick one last time for dessert."

Gabriel couldn't manage stairs yet, couldn't work and couldn't get in the car without a pillow and lying down in the back seat to avoid being sick.

But he was better.

And they were going to be okay.

Chapter Seventeen

Something was not okay.

Chris paused in the open doorway, keys dangling from his fingers and the sweat gluing his shirt to his back. He needed a shower, and to put his shoes to dry on some newspaper. Thunder was growling overhead, but it was nothing compared to the shout that ripped through the house.

"I'm not fucking terminal!"

He relaxed. It wasn't rough sex. Just a row.

Tossing the keys into the bowl, he shut the door and prised off his filthy socks and shoes before heading upstairs. The row was bouncing around in the master bedroom, so he shuffled into the bathroom and turned on the shower. The hint didn't work. They kept shouting as he washed and were no closer to a solution when he stepped out and reached for the nearest towel.

Thing was, Chris couldn't work out what it was about.

He'd never really seen either of them shouting. Gabriel was very placid with him, and if Aled had a temper, Chris simply hadn't been around him long enough to bear witness. And the argument had probably started a while ago, because it seemed to be moving in a loop of Aled saying he wasn't discussing it any further, and Gabriel bawling him out for not discussing it in the first place.

Chris sighed.

Nothing else for it but to interrupt.

He didn't like fights, but the army had given him the tools to deal with it. As a teenager, he'd have been cowering in the corner. As a former squaddie, he just shouldered the bedroom door open and marched in wearing nothing but his towel.

"Can it!" he bellowed.

Silence.

Stunned silence from Gabriel. Aled simply raised an eyebrow.

Gabriel was sat up in bed against a mountain of pillows, a plate of forgotten toast in his lap. Aled was standing by the wardrobe, mostly dressed but for the open collar and undone tie. The lines on his face made him look exhausted, but his mouth was a thin, grim slash.

"What's going on?" Chris asked.

"My—"

"Aled's sister has had her first baby but he's refusing to go and visit because I can't travel yet," Gabriel interrupted. "He's being a fucking moron."

"It doesn't feel right to—"

"She is your *sister*! That baby is your nephew! Your *first* nephew! Go and fucking hold him and send me a cheesy picture, for fuck's sake!"

"They're in Cornwall. I'd have to be gone the whole weekend—"

"Then fucking go!"

"*Oi!*"

Chris had been bullied at school and in the army for being a pussy. He was shy, avoided banter, had never been one of the lads and had usually been taken for gay. But there was one thing he *could* do, and one thing his superior officers had wished he'd do more often.

If he shouted, it put Gunnery Sergeant Hartman to shame.

Gabriel fell mutinously silent, like many a pushy soldier before him, and Chris folded his arms over his chest.

"Aled, go and see your nephew."

Aled pursed his lips.

"And who are you to –"

"I'm the nurse you're literally paying so I can take some of the pressure off," Chris returned. "A couple of days in Cornwall will be good. We can have some time to ourselves, you can relax with your family, everybody wins."

Very pointedly, Aled eyed the bed.

"I'm also the one who has to do most of the lifting and carrying, old man."

"Hey!"

Chris shrugged.

"And what if something happens?"

"Like what?" Chris asked. "Like he falls?"

"Yes. Like he falls."

"Then either he gets up or I call an ambulance. But he's not going to fall, because he can't bribe me with sex into letting him do stupid shit."

Gabriel threw him a foul look, but Chris ignored him.

"Go and meet your baby nephew. We'll be fine, and you need to fucking relax."

"Excuse me —"

"No," Chris snapped. "You look ten years older than last time I was up north. Go and see your goddamn family and stop worrying for five minutes."

"That's easy for you to say. You didn't —"

"Why?"

Aled stopped. Chris raised his eyebrows expectantly.

"Why is it easy for me to say?" he asked, in a far gentler tone. "Because he means more to you? Because it would hurt you more to lose him? You know neither of those are true."

"*He* is right here." But Gabriel's voice, too, was little more than a murmur.

And it worked.

Aled's hard stance softened. His shoulders sagged. The slash in the lower part of his face turned into a mouth again.

"You need some time away," Gabriel said. "We've got this. See Suze, send me twee baby pictures and bitch to her about what a nightmare I am."

Aled huffed a weak laugh. "As always."

"Ring her when you get to work."

Aled checked his watch and rolled his eyes before resuming his wrestle with the tie. "Fine," he said. "You win. But I reserve the right to check in whenever I want."

"If you check in at three in the morning, we're having words," Gabriel retorted.

It took a little more effort to actually get Aled out of the door, and Chris had no doubt he'd want to excuse himself from the evening's making-up routine, but eventually the front door closed and the engine on that enviable car started up. Chris rolled his eyes at the histrionics and headed back upstairs to finish getting dressed.

"I didn't know you and Aled fought," he remarked as Gabriel finally ate his toast.

"Not often," Gabriel admitted. "He's stubborn but he doesn't tend to get loud. That's usually me."

"Was it you this time?"

"Eh, sort of. I got mad, he was frustrated, it all got a bit out of hand." Gabriel waved dismissively. "It happens."

"Never seen *you* shout either."

Gabriel laughed. "That's just you being special."

"Yeah?"

"Mm. You should have heard me when Michael and I were breaking up."

"Who's Michael?"

Chris was treated to a lovely story about a creepy stalker former fuckbuddy, then persuaded to give Gabriel a change of scenery and help him downstairs to the sofa. He could manage the bathroom on his own now — though hot showers were still dicey — and going *up* stairs was working fine, but going down was still too much. He'd get to the third one and start clinging to the banister, white-faced.

Thankfully, he weighed about as much as Chris' racing bike, and carrying him down a flight of stairs was considerably easier than hefting an unwieldy metal frame on and off trains.

"So let me get this straight," he said as they rearranged cushions and tried to find the remote. "Getting the shit kicked out of him by Kevin didn't work, but you cold-cocking him outside a pub did? You're tiny."

"Thanks," Gabriel drawled.

"It's true."

"I think the police had a bit more to do with it. Plus I'd moved in with Aled and lost my job, so I guess I disappeared a little bit. He probably forgot all about me."

"Didn't think stalkers did that."

"Well, he hasn't showed up again," Gabriel said cheerfully. "Hey, so if Aled's going to Cornwall this weekend, we should do something."

"We should also not tell him until he's already sending baby pictures, because I'm not cut out to be a referee in your slanging matches."

"We don't have that many," Gabriel protested.

"Sure."

Chris wasn't dumb. Couples fought. He just didn't want to see it—especially when he wasn't sure whose side he should be on.

"Back on track," Gabriel said. "Let's do something."

"Right," Chris said. "Because I'm going to be persuaded to let you get on a bloody bike."

"Not that kind of something," Gabriel said. "Just—I don't know. Let's go lounge around somewhere that's not the house. Have a fancy spa day or something."

Chris grimaced.

"What? Too manly for a spa day?"

"*Yes.*"

"Nobody's too manly for a spa day," Gabriel retorted. "There's a spa hotel near Halifax that Kevin's taken me to once or twice after some brutal games. The masseuse is *amazing*."

"I can't think of anything less relaxing than a stranger feeling me up," Chris said flatly.

He was already losing the argument, and he knew it. Gabriel wasn't channel-surfing anymore, for one.

"Fine," he said. "I'll take you, but I'm not joining in."

"Not even with the Jacuzzi pool?"

Chris groaned.

"I've heard the hot towel shave is good too," Gabriel continued in that faux-casual tone he adopted whenever he was scheming. "Kevin swears by it."

"Uh-huh."

"So I could have my massage while you get a shave, and we could meet in the pool area…"

"Or I could come and collect you from the massage area so you don't fall on tiles."

"We could bring the wheelchair."

Chris hesitated. The light wheelchair had been abandoned the moment Gabriel got home. He refused to use it, to the point where they did the shopping while he had his midday kip. He wouldn't go out in it, no matter how much Chris bribed and Aled threatened. He'd only done it twice — once for a date with Aled, and once for a mandatory hospital appointment.

Maybe this could be Chris' turn.

"You'll use the chair."

"Yeah."

"You won't argue?"

"No."

"You'll let me take a photo as proof for when Aled finds out and goes insane?"

Gabriel narrowed his eyes. There was a long pause. But eventually he nodded, and Chris sat back against the cushions.

"Fine," he said. "Call your damn hotel."

Chapter Eighteen

The hotel had been the best idea that Gabriel had ever had.

Aled could do a decent massage, but *nothing* beat the lady at the Grand Royal. There was nothing either grand or royal about the old hotel, but both could be liberally applied to Sofia and her magic hands.

By the time Chris came back from his hot shave, ready to take Gabriel to the pool, Gabriel could have dissolved into a puddle. Or died. And he wouldn't have cared which.

Even the vertigo didn't get a look-in over his bliss as Chris helped him down off the massage table and through the warm, steamy corridor to the baths. He sank into the hottest pool in the set, then spread out like a starfish, his head in Chris' hands to anchor him in a haze of happy bliss.

"The phrase 'better than sex' comes to mind," Chris drawled.

"To be fair, this *is* better than most sex."

"Bloody hell. Can I record that?"

"I said most."

"I still want to record that."

Gabriel couldn't even muster up the energy to flip him off.

"Do you feel better?" Chris asked, towing him by the shoulders back to the edge but making no move to right him.

"Mm. Yes."

"Do you maybe want to ring Aled when we're done here and apologise for shouting?"

Gabriel hummed. "He was being over the top."

"Yes. He should apologise too. But you shouldn't have lost your temper."

"Yeah. I suppose."

Gabriel *did* feel a little bad. He knew he had a short fuse at the moment, and Aled hadn't really deserved being screamed at. But the man could be too stubborn for his own good and, at the time, Gabriel hadn't seen a way of being reasonable that would *work*.

Though since when had just yelling worked, either?

"He'll be driving."

"It's called voicemail."

Gabriel hummed. "Yeah. You're right. Once we're done here."

They hadn't booked in to stay the night, just use the facilities for the afternoon. But they were going to get dinner. Gabriel had never been treated to dinner here, but all the online reviews raved about it. He wanted to find out, and apparently the menu was healthy enough to pass muster with Chris.

"I'll call him between this and food."

They had an hour and a half in the baths, and Gabriel floated through every minute of it. The water was almost scalding, and he didn't move a muscle.

Chris came and went to the ice baths and the mid-range pool that dominated the set, but Gabriel remained in the hottest of the hot, feeling every pore open wide and bleed all his anger and tension and shame and negativity out into the water. He'd showered before getting in, obviously, yet he felt as though the water should be black as he pulled himself free at the end of their session. His skin tingled as he scrubbed down in the showers, and he hummed a jaunty tune as he gelled up his hair while waiting for Chris to finish washing.

When he opened the electronic safe at the back of his locker, his phone was waiting on the bottom. Gabriel turned it over, then slipped out of the door into the corridor and leaned up against the wall. Aled would be driving. But—

"Hello?"

He rolled his eyes. "This had better be the hands free."

"Services," Aled replied. He sounded calm. Friendly. It wasn't their first blazing row, and Aled could put on an impressive sulk, but there wasn't a trace of it in his tone and Gabriel relaxed. "Just passed Birmingham. Stopped for a drink. Even with the air conditioning on full, it's nasty out here. Is everything all right?"

Gabriel was impressed he'd left it that long before asking.

"Yeah. Chris and I are at a spa. I feel amazing. Full-body massage and an hour and a half pruning in the hot water."

"You'll look a right sight, then."

"I look beautiful," Gabriel corrected. "So. I'm sorry about earlier."

Aled sighed. "Me too. I was being obstinate."

"I shouldn't have shouted."

"No, you shouldn't. But I should have been prepared to listen."

Gabriel curled his toes in his shoes. "Truce?"

"Truce," Aled agreed. "When I get back, we'll go out and have another cheesy date. I'll pay for dinner, you pay for the cinema tickets. Mutual apologies."

"Then we can kiss and make up in the gents' toilets like a couple of teenagers?"

Aled laughed. "If you want."

"Do you want to see a bad movie so I can blow you in the back and we won't miss anything, or a good movie so we can enjoy it?"

"Mm, let's see what's listed," Aled said. "I'm glad you're feeling better, anyway. You best get back to your spa date with Superman."

"I'll tell him you called him that."

"Terrifying," Aled drawled. Something swooshed, and the faint sound of traffic filtered down the line. "I best hit the road. Thanks for calling."

"Drive safe."

The last remaining bit of tension popped and vanished as he hung up, and Gabriel slipped back into the changing rooms just in time to catch Chris stepping out of the showers with a towel around his waist and water trickling deliciously down his pecs.

"*Why* are you asexual?" Gabriel said mournfully, but behaved himself and sat down to watch instead of pouncing. "I called Aled."

"Made up?"

"Yeah. We're going on a cheesy date when he gets back."

"Didn't think you really did dates anymore."

"What do you call this?"

"With *him*," Chris clarified.

"We do sometimes."

"Aren't they just preludes to your sex games?"

"Well, most of them end up there, sure. But the date itself is still nice," Gabriel said.

"Very romantic."

"It can be. And he pays and I won't put out and…"

"Aaaaand you can stop right there."

Gabriel grinned around his thumbnail, then bit the end of it as Chris dried and dressed. He openly stared, but he was thinking, too.

"Thanks," he said eventually.

"For what?"

"For gluing us back together."

"Come off it. You had an argument. You weren't getting a divorce."

"No, but…you stepped in like you fit. You *do* fit."

He'd joked about them dating and getting to know each other at the beginning, but truth be told, Gabriel hadn't really anticipated Chris slotting in so seamlessly. Aled could be a touch territorial, and Chris more than a touch shy. He hadn't really expected the three of them to work for so long in such close proximity.

"Do you like him?"

"Aled?"

"Yeah."

Chris shrugged. "Sure. Nice guy."

"No, I mean…is it more than that?"

Chris shook his head.

"Huh."

"Why?"

"You—work. I mean, we work. All of us," Gabriel said.

He chewed on his thumbnail as Chris slapped some cologne on, then lifted his arms for a hug before being levered to his feet.

"Drink and dinner?"

"Please," Gabriel said.

"Penny for your thoughts?"

"I'm wondering if this is one big relationship or me in two separate ones," Gabriel admitted.

Although he'd been polyamorous since he'd discovered what fancying other people felt like, he'd never considered any of his relationships joined-up in that sense. He had relationships with Greg and Kevin and Aled and Chris—but none of them had relationships with each other, too. He'd never been in a triad, just a few very sexy threesomes. If he were to draw them in a diagram, he'd be a blob radiating straight lines in every direction, but none of those lines ever joining to one another.

Except for now.

With Chris in the same house, interfering in their row, getting Gabriel to make amends...

He was involved in a way nobody else had been. Sure, Kevin and Aled swapped him over now and then, and he knew from a few pouncings where one or the other had mysterious knowledge of his whereabouts that they talked behind his back, but they never went for drinks together. Aled didn't come round for dinner with Kevin and Judith and the kids. They knew each other, but there wasn't really any kind of relationship between them.

There was one between Aled and Chris.

They'd gone out for a drink and dinner of their own while Gabriel was recovering. They ganged up on him occasionally. They talked without him sat in the middle. Chris hadn't bothered trying to move back into the spare room.

Chris might not fancy Aled, and Aled probably didn't fancy Chris either, but there was some kind of friendship there. A relationship. More than any of Gabriel's other boyfriends had ever had between them.

Had his accident created a triad?

"Do you and Aled still go on dates?"

Chris snorted. "You what?"

"You know, your curry date when I had dinner at Kevin's, and—"

"Sure. If you want to call 'em dates, then yeah. We've had a couple of dates."

"Maybe you should talk about your future on the third date."

"Don't push your luck," Chris warned.

They'd reached the restaurant. Gabriel flirted their way to a table in the conservatory overlooking the gardens. Chris called him shameless once the waiter had retreated to get their drinks.

But the thought lingered.

He hadn't meant to do it, and he was sure that they were hardly aware of it themselves, but their V shape was closing into a triangle.

Chapter Nineteen

Cornwall was pretty in the long summer twilight.

Tom had taken up a position on the board of his father's hotel firm last year, but Suze hadn't wanted to actually live in one of the hotels and had insisted on getting their own place. In the end, they'd bought a little house on the outskirts of St Ives, with an optimistic — given that Tom had about twenty siblings — two extra bedrooms for housing their future offspring.

It was buried in a nest of small, twisting residential streets, and Aled still relied on the satnav to get him to the right cul-de-sac, but the moment his car turned into the mouth of the street, a front door opened. Blonde hair flashed. He had barely stopped the car before Suze opened his door, leaned in and hugged him in a death-defying chokehold.

"Oh my God, *hello!*"

"Hey," he coughed.

Suze and Aled were the same age, though she looked infinitely better for it than he did. They'd grown up round the corner from one another as children and had been lifelong friends. In effect, Suze was his sister. And with her ash-blonde hair, fair complexion and post-baby belly, she could even pass for the real thing.

But more than looks or history, her hold was like coming home. Her familiar perfume. The way her hair tickled his nose. The exact timbre of her voice. Aled closed his eyes and basked for a long minute, just holding on to the one person left in his life who he considered family. His parents were gone, his nan had passed, but his sister was still here.

"Come on! Come and meet your nephew!"

And his family was growing again. Aled allowed her to drag him out of the car and had to fight to be permitted to bring his bag instead of being bullied straight into the house. He didn't really care all that much about seeing the baby — Aled was about as child-friendly as the measles — but the warm familiarity of their house, the same pictures on the wall they'd had in Yorkshire, the booming hello from his brother-in-law —

Everything else just fell away.

The accident, the row, Gabriel's health, how Chris was fitting into their lives, whether his boss was going to let him out of the upcoming conference in the US...

None of it mattered in the middle of Suze's hall.

"Drop that!" she said, smacking his hand on his suitcase. "Tom'll sort it later. Come and meet Euan!"

Euan.

After Aled's dad, who'd been a father to Suze as much as he had to Aled. An affable, laid-back man who'd adopted his best friend's orphaned son and made sure he never felt the lack of blood relation between them. The calm presence in Aled's upbringing, who'd puffed away on his cigarettes in the background while Aled had been figuring out who he was and what he wanted to do with himself. The man with the stiff upper lip over minor crises, but who'd shaken and openly cried at his wife's funeral, at the loss of Aled's grandfather, at Aled's graduation, at Aled's wedding. The gentle but firm hand that had steered him, and the constant security that had said Aled could make mistakes, could fail, could be a billionaire or a binman, and it wouldn't make any difference. His father would still be proud of him, and his mother would still adore him.

The name still brought a lump to Aled's throat.

Only briefly, though. Euan *was* a lump. Four days old, he looked like an oversized blood clot in a fluffy jumper. He was in a Moses basket on the kitchen table, and the only resemblance Aled could see to anyone on earth was the tiny wisps of brown hair. He'd always wondered if saying new babies looked like their parents wasn't a bit of a backhanded compliment, and Euan's squashed, ugly face confirmed it. Hopefully he'd grow into the nose.

"Cute," he said lamely.

"Hold him!"

"Oh, God. Really? Do I have to?"

Suze punched him in the arm until he sat down, then the blood clot was deposited in his clumsy arms. Immediately, a gob like the Channel Tunnel opened and a shriek that could kill a man at a hundred paces emerged. Then Tom settled the clot's head against Aled's elbow, and it mercifully shut up again.

"Aww, he likes you!"

"Great," Aled said, and promptly ignored the clot in favour of Suze. "How are you doing?"

"I'm fine," she said. "The midwife was amazing. I'm still struggling to breastfeed a little bit, but he likes formula so it's not too bad."

"How's trying to sleep?"

"She sleeps when he sleeps," Tom drawled, plunking a cup of coffee down in front of Aled. "I sleep at work."

Aled chuckled. He managed to give the baby back in exchange for his coffee and relaxed into his chair as he watched Suze coddle her newborn son. She'd waited years to have him — finding the right father, finding enough money, getting married — and though Aled couldn't understand wanting a baby for the life of him, he had to admit that she looked...right. She looked good with him. Something had settled over her, something a little deeper than just happiness.

"Being a mum suits you," he murmured.

She beamed at him.

"So if he's Euan, is your daughter going to be Anjali?"

She laughed. "I don't think we'd get away with that. Actually, we were thinking Amanda or Noah for the next one. But it won't be for a few years. I want Euan to be old enough to understand about getting a baby brother or sister, not be jealous."

"Well, I think you're mad for even having one, but you do you," Aled remarked.

"Oh, shove off," Suze said. "Baby hater. Hasn't Gabriel persuaded you into having kids yet?"

"I don't think there's enough money in the world to persuade Gabriel to have a baby," Aled said. "Anyway, I'm safe. Can't produce the goods, remember?"

Suze freed one hand to flip him the bird.

"You can have enough babies for the both of us."

"Only two!"

Aled raised his eyebrows at Tom, who just shrugged.

"I just get what I'm given," he said. "Speaking of which, give it here."

"*Him*!" Suze squawked.

"Could be a girl."

"Well, until he says that, he's a he," she said primly, but let Tom take the blood clot away. It—he—howled again and grumbled away in his Moses basket for a few more minutes to let the peasants know of his displeasure before Tom picked said basket up and disturbed the peace once more.

"I'll get his lordship bathed and in the cot," he said. "You two girls have a good catch up."

"Fuck off," Aled said lightly.

"Same to you, knobhead."

Aled relaxed back in his chair once the hand grenade of a baby had been removed, and eyed Suze appraisingly. She looked a little rough around the edges, but no worse than a lazy weekend at home.

"You look good," he repeated. "It suits you."

She softened. "Thank you. It's hard, but it's amazing, too."

"I'm pleased for you."

"Thank you." Then she tapped his wrist. "How's Gabriel doing? I'm so sorry I wasn't able to come and see him in hospital. Is he—"

"He's doing fine, and he understands," Aled said. "All the broken bones have healed fine, and he's putting some of the weight back on. Migraines seemed to have tapered off, too. The main problem is the vertigo."

"Still bad?"

"We had a bit of a row," he admitted. "I wasn't too happy about coming down on my own. I suggested delaying it until he was up to the journey and he ripped me a new one."

"Good!"

"He'll be down once he can travel long distance. Cars still make him throw up. And he can't take stairs on his own yet. And a hot shower is a real health hazard. But—" He waved a hand. "He's...you know. It could have been worse."

She squeezed his hand.

"And how are *you* doing?"

"Honestly? Chris has been a massive help," Aled admitted. "He'd make a good nurse. Totally unflappable. Just takes everything in his stride, and he keeps Gabriel on the level too. He's doing miles better than I would on my own."

"So how's living with him?" Suze asked. "You used to get so twitchy about having his boyfriends in the house."

"That was walking in on sex, and not really any fear of that with Chris."

"Mm, good point."

"But no, it's fine. I think I might have really conquered that one."

It had been one of his hangovers from his marriage. Although Aled wasn't naturally jealous, he did insist on knowing what was going on. The line—for him—between an open relationship and being cheated on was the knowledge. And while Melissa had been generally on board, there'd been an incident or two of walking in the door and, with no warning, finding another man balls-deep in his wife. And all the openness in the world hadn't stopped Aled from blowing his lid.

So when Gabriel had moved in, there'd been an uneasy few months where they were stuck between a rock and a hard place. Gabriel's gender made anonymous hotel room sex with new playthings dangerous sometimes. But Aled's hangup about having other men in the house had locked the door on the obvious option of bringing them into familiar territory with someone else nearby to prevent problems. It had taken time to unknot Aled's twitchiness, and more patience than Gabriel usually showed, but—

Well, he knew full well Chris had shagged him at least once in there.

"There's not really any strangers anymore anyway," he admitted. "He's settled down a bit lately. It's just been me, Kevin, Chris and that Greg guy from the gym when there's been a good gig on."

"The Leeds Arena toilets guy?"

"Yeah."

"Is he helping out?"

"Nah. He's just a fuckbuddy," Aled said. "And he's nice enough, but he's got the intelligence of a teaspoon. Not sure I'd *want* him trying to help out."

Suze laughed and called him a snob before asking how long Chris was going to stay.

"Until Gabriel doesn't need constant supervision. Whenever that is."

"Why not permanently?" Suze asked.

Aled hummed. "I—I don't know, Suze. He's a nice guy, but—all the time? I'm not sure I'm really up for a permanent roommate."

"But Gabriel might be. He's not really enjoyed the constant back and forth between Bristol and Wakefield, has he?"

"No, but he doesn't do it that often. They usually go biking somewhere else and stay in a hostel or a B&B."

"I'm just saying you should think about it," Suze said. "There's more room in your new house. Or you could help him find a flat or something nearby, so he's more local but not in your space all the time."

"That's up to him," Aled demurred. "He's never shown any interest in moving north before. Bit of a southern nancy."

"Hey! You watch what you say about southerners."

"Cornwall's not southern. It's a foreign country."

"*Rude.*"

"True," he countered. "How else do you explain Tom? He's almost an alien."

"Are you saying my son is a creature from outer space?"

"Basically."

She hit him, he argued that he was right, and the serious discussion dissolved — as they always did with Suze — into a childish argument with a lifelong friend.

But she'd planted an idea in the back of his mind, and it ticked over even as they argued, changed the subject, had more tea and ate in front of the TV. It stayed, itching at his brain.

What if Chris stayed?

What if he didn't?

Aled wasn't entirely sure what the right answer was anymore.

Chapter Twenty

Chris was woken from a leisurely Sunday afternoon doze by Gabriel's phone chiming and reached for it on instinct. Gabriel stirred sleepily, still sprawled over Chris' body, and merely opened one eye to peer at the screen when Chris handed it over.

"Aled's staying another day in St Ives," he mumbled, then dropped the phone on Chris' shoulder.

"S'fine." Chris yawned. "Okay. Dinner. Let me up."

"Let me help?"

"If you can sit at the table without falling off the chair."

Gabriel mocked his accent. It took a couple of tries to get him off the sofa, and he swayed dangerously for a minute or two, but the walk to the kitchen was stable and he slid down into one of the chairs like nothing was wrong.

"Vegetarian enchiladas?"

"Murdered cow enchiladas."

Chris rolled his eyes but got a packet of mince out of the fridge.

"And don't scrimp on the cheese," Gabriel added, propping his head on his fist with a heavy yawn. "Maybe it's a good thing Aled's coming back tomorrow. I'm too tired for sex."

"Can I record you saying that?"

Gabriel flipped him off.

"I didn't think Aled liked babies," Chris admitted.

"He doesn't."

"But he's voluntarily spending time with a baby."

"With his nephew."

Chris snapped his fingers, reminded by the word.

"Is it *actually* his nephew?" he said. "I thought Suze was his friend, not his sister."

"I mean, sure, biologically speaking, she's nothing to do with him," Gabriel said. "But they've been best friends since they were little kids, and he gave her away at her wedding. Her family are shit, I think. Her dad or her brother or someone like that is in prison and her mum is one of those no-go areas of discussion. So Aled's basically her brother in everything but blood. She used to visit his nan in the nursing home, too. I think she's named the baby after Aled's dad."

"You think?"

"Euan. I think that was Aled's dad's name. He died years ago," Gabriel added. "Long before me and Aled got together. I think it wasn't long after Aled got married, actually."

"Still weirds me out to think of Aled with a wife," Chris admitted.

He'd seen a photo in one of the bedroom drawers — a much younger and slimmer Aled, with hair like the Great Fire of London, beaming in his penguin suit with a pretty girl on his arm, reddish-blonde hair cascading down her shoulders in artful curls. He'd seen the *evidence.* But it didn't quite click. Aled had been someone's husband. Husbands wore knitted jumpers and waited with the bags in shopping centres. Aled was about as far from Chris' mental picture of a husband as it was possible to get.

"They were really young. She was his first girlfriend—like, secondary school level first girlfriend. He was absolutely besotted with her."

At least Chris could see the besotted side of things.

"So what happened?"

Gabriel shrugged. "She wanted a baby."

"Ahh," Chris said.

He wasn't exactly an authority on relationships, but even he knew the odds of sustaining a marriage when one wanted children and the other didn't.

"Turns out Aled can't have kids, so she left him."

"*Ouch.*"

"Mm."

"Wait, he can't?"

"Nope. I mean, he doesn't want them either, but turns out he literally can't." Gabriel flashed him a grin. "Means I can usually persuade him to abandon the condoms."

Chris frowned. Why—

"Why would that make a difference?"

Gabriel blinked. "Um, because he can't get me pregnant anyway?"

"But...but you can't get pregnant."

There was a long pause.

"Er."

Sweat prickled under Chris' arms. Oh shit. Oh *shit.*

"Oh my God, you can get pregnant."

"Well...yeah," Gabriel said slowly. "I mean, I have ovaries."

"Holy shit."

He'd never thought about it properly. He knew what Gabriel *had*, obviously. He'd—you know. Seen things. Touched them. Not the *ovaries*—that would be insane—but other...evidence. But Gabriel didn't get periods, and surely that was enough, right?

He said as much, and Gabriel began to laugh.

"Well, it lowers the odds, but it's not impossible," he said. "What are you so worried about? You always use a condom."

"Not *always*!" Chris protested. "Not that time in Snowdonia!"

"We'd have a one-year-old if you'd got me pregnant in Snowdonia," Gabriel said flippantly. "Anyway, even if you did knock me up, I'm not having a baby. No way in hell."

Chris squirmed, fidgeting with the spatula. He wanted to ask—and especially while Gabriel was in a good mood and appeared open to questions—but he wasn't entirely sure he wanted to know. Chris wasn't exactly comfortable discussing...bodies.

"Has it...you know. Ever happened?"

"Twice," Gabriel said.

"Oh." He coughed. "Um. Who?"

"Some hookup, can't remember his name. And don't know about the other one."

Chris shivered at the mental image of Gabriel with a baby belly.

"I do not want kids."

"Good, because you're not getting any here," Gabriel said. "I like babies fine, but I'm not hefting one around in my guts for nine months then shoving it out in front of half a hospital. I can get all my baby fix from cuddling Kevin's kids when I go to visit. And now

Euan. And you can hand them back when they shit themselves or they start crying. I just get them when they're all cute and sleepy and smell like talcum powder."

"Yeah, well, you're welcome to them," Chris said, poking the simmering chilli meat. "Adults are hard enough to handle. Children are just—no. No way in hell."

"Agreed," Gabriel said, but when Chris looked over his shoulder, he was being offered a shit-eating grin. "Did you seriously not realise I could get knocked up?"

Chris felt his face flame red, and it was nothing to do with the proximity of the pan.

"I—I assumed that...well, come on. You have a *beard*. Don't your hormones stop that kind of thing?"

"Most of the time, yeah. But it's not foolproof. Plenty of trans men have been knocked up when they were on hormones. And my dose is pretty low, so I've definitely been spitting out eggs now and again. I had a period last Christmas out of nowhere. It happens."

"Oh, *ew*."

"You are so gay," Gabriel chuckled.

"I just don't like the whole...pregnancy deal."

"Well, last I checked you had two bollocks and no vagina, so I wouldn't worry about it too much."

"*Thank* you," Chris grumbled.

"Welcome," Gabriel said in the brightest, most obnoxious tone possible.

"You're a dick," Chris muttered. The fierce heat in his face was going absolutely nowhere. "It's been a long time since sex education lessons in school, okay? And I haven't exactly been...revising."

"Revising," Gabriel echoed. "Oh my God."

"Shut up!"

Gabriel did—briefly, with some sniggering—and Chris concentrated on dinner to try and quell the embarrassment. He could barely remember sex education in school, and he was certain there'd been no lessons on whether trans people had babies. Or that trans people even *existed*. He had a vague memory of everyone sniggering as they tried to put condoms on bananas, and some lurid purple diagram of the female reproductive system. That was about it.

"We've—you've never—"

"You never got me pregnant. Snowdonia or otherwise."

"Would you have told me if I had?" he asked.

"Dunno," Gabriel admitted. "I mean, I'd have got rid of it anyway. I might have told *you*—always figured you'd not like babies—but...I wouldn't have told Greg if he did it. I'd only tell Kevin on the proviso he wouldn't tell his wife. She's *really* anti-abortion."

Chris wrinkled his nose.

"Yeah."

"Urgh. Who's Greg?"

"The guy I went to the Placebo gig with."

"Oh, the gym guy."

"Yeah."

"So—" Chris turned down the burner and slid into the seat opposite Gabriel at the little table, mustering up his most serious expression and looking Gabriel dead in the eye. "Just so we're absolutely clear. No kids."

Gabriel laughed. "No kids."

"Okay. Thank you."

He went back to the pan, followed by Gabriel's amused voice.

"You sound *terrified*. You realise growing a baby inside your own body is something that about half the population can do?"

"Yeah, the half I've never slept with."

"Please, you've jizzed in me like...what, twice? Three times? I've had more cum out of some of my one-time-only hookups. I'd have to be Judith to get pregnant from you."

"Judith?"

"Kevin's wife. They have three daughters under six, and she's about to drop a fourth."

"Oh my God."

"Lily and Grace are literally ten months apart. They're lucky they won't be in the same school year."

"Does Kevin have a pregnancy fetish?" Chris blurted out, the thought escaping before he could catch it and stuff it back into the recesses of his terrified brain.

"I think it's Judith, actually. He keeps complaining she won't let him wear a rubber. She wants six kids."

"Holy fuck. No. No-no-no-no."

Gabriel cackled.

"Is she mad?"

"Probably. She did marry Kevin."

"And they're, uh. You know. Kinky?"

"Very."

Chris shivered as he warmed the tortillas. "I didn't even know you could have sex with a pregnant lady."

"Oh my God, where *did* you go to school?"

"Fucking Somerset, all right? You—you know. You do it like sheep down there. Four minutes and it's over and you get a baby."

"I don't even know where to start with how backward that is," Gabriel said.

"And the army is just wall-to-wall knob jokes."

"The army *is* a wall-to-wall knob joke," Gabriel retorted.

Chris ignored him to add the chilli and cheese and perfect his creations. Thinking about pregnant sex while melting cheese into peppers, chilli beef and a liberal supply of salsa wasn't a good idea. His stomach was already rebelling.

"Honestly, no wonder it took so long before you tried to take my trousers off," Gabriel said as dinner was served. "I'm beginning to think I'm privileged that you even want to get near me."

"And for that remark, you're not getting any for a week."

"*Rude.*"

Of course, that wasn't how Chris' life worked. Even though they changed the subject and talked about a potential trip to Scarborough once Gabriel was able to travel decent distances in the car again, his dick had taken an interest in proceedings. By the time he was washing up, that aggravating pulse had started. And so, despite his bruised ego, they ended up watching a horror movie in bed, Gabriel's hopefully infertile body warm around his cock, and a condom nicked from Aled's stash in the bathroom keeping any more baby talk at bay.

It was over quickly, and Gabriel peeled the used condom off before distracting Chris from the stomach-turning revulsion with a quick kiss and a sharp tug on his ear.

"There you go," he said. "No babies. Now get out of my way. I want to see who dies first."

Chris dragged himself off. Gabriel cuddled up under his arm. It was a shitty film from the early 2000s, so the black guy died first. Chris' dick went back to sleep, and the unease settled under a layer of warmth that was nothing to do with the duvet, and everything to do with the dead weight giving him pins and needles along his left arm.

"Gabriel?"

"Ssh!"

"Love you."

"I said *ssh*."

But then a foot rubbed up against his own under the covers, and the tiny pressure on his collarbone might have been a kiss.

"Love you, too."

Chapter Twenty-One

Gabriel was almost there.

He could have proper sex. The wheelchair had been given back to the hospital. He could drift in a hot pool until his skin dissolved. Getting dressed didn't make him fall back into bed the minute he tried to put on socks or pull a shirt over his head. He could — as long as he was lying down — ride in a car without throwing up. He could even walk round to the shop with Chris at lunchtime and sneak a doughnut when the health freak wasn't looking. Even that cunt of a consultant had referred him back to his GP and taken him off everything but the migraine medication and the as-and-when painkillers in case the skull fracture acted up.

He was so fucking *close*.

But there was one thing standing between Gabriel and being *better*.

He stood in the bathroom doorway, staring at the stairs, and felt wobbly just thinking about them.

"Give me a minute," Chris said through a beard of shaving foam. "Won't be long with this."

"'Kay," Gabriel said, but didn't take his eyes off the stairs. They wavered as if they were underwater. When he blinked, they shivered.

He'd not once managed getting down them on his own. Up was bad, but not impossible. With supervision, or if he crawled on hands and knees like a little kid, he could get *up* the stairs. But down? No. Something about going down the stairs — any stairs — made the vertigo a thousand times worse. What had dulled into a gentle tug around the ears most of the time, and even vanished entirely when he was sitting down or lying in the hammock, rose into the tipping deck of a sailing ship in a hurricane whenever he tried to tackle stairs. One step worked. Two started to shake. And on the third, he would sag into Chris' grasp and cling to him to be carried the rest of the way. Usually crying in frustration.

He hated it.

Hated it.

And yet he couldn't get past it. He'd been trying every morning for three weeks to conquer them, and it just wasn't working.

But today —

Today there was a flicker of hope. Not from the vertigo, which seemed to have hit its limit and hadn't improved in a while, but from a conversation. When Gabriel had complained over breakfast about being stuck on one floor of the house, Chris had made a suggestion about where to look.

"I get dizzy with ear infections," he'd said. "I always found it helped to do that gymnast thing. You know, stare into the middle distance?"

Gabriel stared down the shaking steps, then raised his eyes to the wall.

The stairs in the old house had curved to fit, but in the new house they fell in a long, straight line down into the living room. He could just about see the edge of the sofa from the landing, and the sofa was his goal. He wanted to walk downstairs, sit on the sofa and watch a film with Chris with their feet up on the coffee table.

The stairs themselves were the only thing throwing a wrench in the works.

A wooden banister supported one side, and the wall the other. They'd taken out the railing drilled into the wall for being ugly, but Gabriel regretted the decision now. He could have done with a white-knuckle grip on both. As it was, he was tempted to lean up against the wall to slide his way down.

"Okay." The tap switched off. "Ready. You want carrying, or—"

"I want to try it myself first," Gabriel said.

To Chris' credit, he didn't argue. "Uh, okay. Let me go first, then."

Gabriel kept his eyes trained on the opposite wall as he inched towards the stairs. He was barefoot, and the lush carpet cuddled his toes before he took that first step off the edge of the abyss and lowered his weight through the wind buffeting his brain. His body hung in the vacuum of space. The cold wall under his palm tipped downwards. The banister shook.

But he kept his eyes on the opposite wall, and his foot met carpet once more.

"Fuck," he muttered.

"Just take your time."

"I'm gonna do this."

"On your own time."

He didn't dare nod. Instead, he clung to the banister as he slid the second foot down to join the first and steeled himself to do it again.

The second time was just as bad, but the awful wait with his feet on different levels was shorter. Once he could press his ankles together like two sides of a jigsaw and locked his knees, the sensation of something shadowy grabbing at him and trying to pull him over eased.

He kept his eyes on the wall and slid his hands down for the third try.

He'd never made it this far on his own before, and when his foot touched the third step, his vision began to blur with tears. He blinked them away to keep focus on the wall and they ran down his face in hot streaks.

"You okay?" Chris murmured.

"Yeah."

"You're doing great."

"M'gonna do it," he croaked.

He was going to do it. He was going to walk down the fucking stairs. He *was*.

His knee buckled on the fourth, but Gabriel clung to the banister and forced himself upright again. He closed his eyes rather than look down, and the terrifying sensation of a sheer drop faded. After a little while of hugging his ankles together, the newfound nausea abated too, and he tried for the fifth.

And the sixth.

And the *seventh*.

Slowly, the wall gave away to the living room ceiling and he focused on the light fitting instead. On the swirly patterns that had presumably been the fashion for plasterers all over Yorkshire when the house was built. Sweat was running down his back. His hands were shaking with the effort of holding on. He wasn't entirely sure which way was up, and his stomach was rebelling worse than its puking sessions in the hospital. He was going to hurl.

Only he was on the eighth step.

The ninth.

The ceiling got too high, and he focused on the window instead, warm summer sun streaming in from the road. There was a butterfly dancing on the outside of the glass and he stared at it until the colours blurred into an indistinct blob. He was going to sit in the sun. He was going to lounge in the sun until it moved around to the other side of the house, then he was going to get into the hammock and read a book or something.

Ten steps.

Eleven.

"Gabriel."

"In a minute," he croaked. His feet hurt. Knees. Hips. *Everything* hurt, aching with the tension that vibrated down his whole body like a plucked violin string. His heart was pounding in his chest. His hair was damp at the temples and around his ears. He needed another shower. God, he was going to have to turn right around and go straight back up—

"Look down."

"No."

"Look *down.*"

Chris' hand squeezed his wrist. Gabriel glanced at him.

And frowned.

Not—

Not *down* at him. Chris was level with him. Chris was—

Gabriel looked down.

A single solitary step stood between him and the living room rug.

"One more," Chris said, and held open his arms. "C'mere."

The vertigo clawed at Gabriel's brain. His vision was both perfectly fine and perfectly fucked. He wanted to puke. He wanted to fall. Collapse in a heap and forget he was human. Forget that a flight of fucking *stairs* had reduced him to such a mess.

Instead, he burst into tears.

As he stepped off the edge of the planet into Chris' arms.

Chapter Twenty-Two

Aled put his keys in the door, then yelped as it was jerked back and Gabriel flung his arms around his neck.

"Um. Hello?"

"I walked down the stairs!"

Aled laughed. "On your own?"

"Yes!"

He grinned, seized Gabriel's face for a kiss then picked him up and twirled. That earned a shriek and a protest — and a little clinginess when he stopped — but it was worth it for the sunny beam on Gabriel's face.

"Twice," Gabriel enthused. "I did it twice. Chris didn't need to help once. I can do *stairs*. I'm getting better!"

He *looked* better too. The sun had come up in his eyes. A flash of arousal smashed through Aled's body, and he grabbed a handful of hair to kiss him again. Open. Hungry. *Biting.*

Gabriel whimpered and fingers tangled in his belt. The buckle slid free.

"Do it again," he whispered when Aled let go of his hair and mouth.

Aled backed him into the wall, biting at his neck. Gabriel shuddered. Whined. His hands seized Aled's love handles and pulled him closer. He opened his legs around Aled's hips and ground up against his dick. Still soft, but not for long. Aled dropped his briefcase. Groped blindly to slam the front door. He could go for anything—a wall fuck, a worship, a wank into an unwilling body...

The latter made itself known. The sudden squirm. The attempt to close open thighs. Gabriel pulled away from the kiss and whimpered when Aled sank his teeth into his shoulder instead.

"Wait—"

Aled ignored him. The hot summer wasn't abating, and Gabriel was only wearing a pair of denim shorts and a baggy T-shirt. And not for long. Aled ripped the T-shirt off over his head and bit again, this time on a puffy nipple. Gabriel had small breasts, and Aled could almost fit the whole swell into his mouth. He sucked until Gabriel tried to push him off, then let go to grip Gabriel's jaw in one hand and crush him into silence.

"If you're fit enough to climb the stairs, you're fit enough to lie on your back and open your legs," he said.

"Later?" Gabriel pleaded. "Your friend is still here. I can't—please. Not in front of your friend."

"You think I'm stupid?" Aled said. "You've been alone in the house with him for weeks. There's no way a whore like you hasn't been gagging on his cock for breakfast every morning."

"I haven't!"

"Bullshit," Aled said. "I know he's fucked you. He's seen you moan like a bitch in heat before — what do you care if he sees you do it again?"

He let go, only to seize Gabriel by the upper arms and frogmarch him into the living room, topless with pink bites decorating his neck and nipples. Chris was sitting in the corner, bike upended on some newspaper, and stared.

"Stay and watch, or clear off," Aled said. "Doesn't matter to me."

He immediately flung Chris out of his mind, focusing instead on throwing Gabriel down on the sofa and ripping those tiny shorts down his legs. His underwear followed, then Aled stepped back and dropped his trousers. He stepped out of them, unbuttoned the fly on his boxers and drew out his cock, pumping it quickly to hardness.

"So how do you want it?" he asked. "You going to ride me like a lover, or do you want to be fucked like the free slut you are?"

Gabriel fisted his hands into the cushions. Even through the roleplay, Aled could see the indecision. Be humiliated by being taunted as he sat in Aled's lap and wriggled, having his tits played with like he was nothing more than a sex doll? Or be held down and pounded until Aled gagged him with his own underwear to muffle the screaming?

Aled waited, wanking idly, until Gabriel's throat bobbed and he finally offered an answer.

"I — I'll ride you."

"Ask nicely."

Gabriel's face burned red. "Can — can I ride your cock, sir?"

Aled smirked and sat down on the end of the sofa, patting his thigh.

"Come on, then. Put your lips around it. Any lips."

He'd appreciate the blowjob, but Gabriel seemed to want it deeper than that. He crawled over Aled's lap, looping his arms around Aled's neck to steady himself, and the warm wetness of his pussy gently kissed the head of Aled's dick before he began to lower himself.

"*Fuuuuck*," Aled breathed.

The tight heat that sank over him was glorious. He dropped his head back with a deep, guttural groan.

"God, I could fuck that cunt all day," he murmured. "You're still tight for a two-timing whore."

Gabriel settled into his lap, fully-seated, and wasted no time. His hips rolled forwards, and Aled's cock was massaged, squeezed, almost milked, by a very talented body.

"Very nice." Aled slapped his arse, enjoying the jolt both inside and outside, then cupped bouncing tits in both hands and squeezed until a look of pain crossed Gabriel's face. He relaxed his grip, then leaned forward to take the nipple ring between his teeth. He pulled until Gabriel cried out, then let go with a laugh. "I'm going to get you a chain for that. You'd like that, wouldn't you? Getting pulled around by your tits."

"N-no. It hurts. Please —"

"You get off on pain." Aled squeezed his breasts again and bucked his hips up into Gabriel's. "Hear that? It's like fucking a bowl of water. You're dripping. Tight as a drum and you didn't need a single lick to lube you up."

Then he let go.

Sat back.

Draped his arms over the back of the sofa.

His own orgasm was a while away yet, but Gabriel was leaking around him like a burst pipe and the flushed heat in his face and neck wasn't entirely the humiliation of being dirty-talked in front of his other boyfriend.

"Fuck yourself," Aled said.

"B-but—"

"No touching your own. You ride my dick until you come," Aled instructed. "You've got ten minutes. And if you don't—"

He leaned forward until his lips brushed Gabriel's ear.

"Then I'll put this up your arse and you can come like that instead."

* * * *

Half an hour later, Gabriel was face down on the sofa with Aled's belt securing his arms behind his back, gagged with his own briefs and being fucked in long, hard, painful thrusts.

And he screamed with every single one, because he'd disobeyed.

He'd brought himself close several times in his allocated ten minutes, but had eventually jacked off. Aled had let him, holding the base of his own dick so he wouldn't be jerked off by Gabriel's powerful orgasms, and had then turned him over, trussed him up and fingered him until he was ready for something more considerable.

It didn't stop him screaming, though.

It hadn't stop him coming a second time, either, and Aled was looking forward to the third one. He always tried for a third. It was the ultimate humiliation, making Gabriel jack off while Aled fingered the cum back out of him.

Although—

He glanced up as he fucked.

Chris was still watching.

Aled had expected him to leave or try to interfere out of ignorance about their games. But he must have picked up on the lack of safewords, and he was still staring. Not quite as pale and stunned as when it had all started, but—

Aled's gaze dropped.

He was hard.

Interesting.

As he pulled out, Aled caught Chris' eye once more and smirked. The cyclist sat perfectly still on the cuddle chair, knuckles white where he was gripping the armrests. The hard-on in his jeans was clearly visible. His bike had long since been abandoned.

"I think my friend wants to have a go," Aled murmured in Gabriel's ear, just loud enough for Chris to hear, and tugged the underwear gag free. "Let's put you to better use, shall we?"

"N-no—" Gabriel whimpered.

"If he wants, then he gets."

"But—"

"Sluts don't get a choice," Aled purred. "And we both know what you are. Say it."

Gabriel whined.

"*Say it.*"

He rolled his hips again. Even the hint of the threat was enough.

"I'm a slut."

"And?"

"And—and y-your friend wants to fuck me."

"So?"

"S-so he gets to."

"Because?"

"Because s-sluts don't get a choice."

"Much better," Aled said and squeezed both cheeks in his hands until he left fingerprints. He still ached to come there, but an interesting prospect beckoned instead. "My friend prefers it dry. So he can pump a load into you, and you can put your mouth to better use than whining about it. How does that sound?"

"G-good. Sir."

"Much better."

He climbed off the sofa, and Chris was up off the chair in a matter of seconds. His jeans hit the floor. Aled smirked before schooling his expression and yanked on Gabriel's hair to get him on his hands and knees.

"Get on with it, then," he said, perching on the arm of the chair.

He wasn't kind about it. Gabriel tried to suck gently on the head, but Aled forced his head down until he gagged on far too much hard cock, then yelled when Chris roughly entered him from behind with a harsh slap of flesh on flesh. Aled groaned as the impact shivered down his dick. He'd only done a threesome with Gabriel twice before, and Suze's gay brother-in-law didn't have nearly the same hard, cruel appearance that Chris did. Daz looked almost sweet. Chris looked like — like —

Like exactly the kind of cunt that an abusive master *would* whore his sex toys out to.

Chris fucked him rough and fast, hands gripping Gabriel's hips and fucking into him so hard that Aled didn't bother to thrust. He just held a fistful of Gabriel's hair and let Chris do the work from the other end,

Gabriel's whimpers muffled and occasionally entirely silenced by Aled's cock. And when it got too much, when things started to darken —

Aled yanked, pulled out and came on Gabriel's face.

It was a brutal climax, and it left him breathless and with a handful of loose hair in his fist. Gabriel gasped for breath, sobbing as Chris continued to fuck him, and Aled laughed coldly, tugging on the rumpled black spikes again.

"Clean it off, then."

"Y-yes, sir —"

His dick was too sensitive for sucking, but the soft laps of Gabriel's tongue and the sight of his cum drying on those delicate features was almost like a second orgasm. When Chris finally groaned and — by the sudden stutter of movement — came, Gabriel dropped his head to sob, and Aled casually slid a hand under his throat to squeeze until he looked up.

"What do you say?"

"T-thank you, sir."

"And?"

"Thank you, Mr Wheeler."

Chris raised his eyebrows at the title but said nothing. He pulled out. Gabriel grimaced, and Aled grinned as Chris followed his cue and smacked his arse with an open hand before getting up and walking out like nothing had happened.

"You need to practice," Aled said. "Don't you agree?"

It was a mixture of threat and question. A natural out without disturbing the atmosphere if Gabriel murmured a colour instead of an answer. A way of easing them back down without the shuddering halt of slamming on the brakes.

But when Gabriel answered, it was plain as day that Aled wasn't the only one who didn't want to come down yet.

"Yes, sir."

"Good," Aled murmured, and worried at that exposed, vulnerable throat once more. "Now, be a good little cumslut and crawl upstairs to get your toys for me."

Chapter Twenty-Three

Chris shut himself in the bathroom, turned on the shower…and sank down onto the toilet.

He had no idea what had just happened.

Well, no, he *did*. He'd fucked Gabriel from behind while he was gagged with Aled's hard dick. He'd screwed him like something out of a porn movie. He'd come so hard he'd nearly blacked out, and he'd watched Aled fuck it right back out of Gabriel in even harder thrusts.

Chris knew perfectly well what had happened factually.

But why the hell had he joined in?

Usually if they'd started to play while Chris was around, he would have just walked out. Aled was normally pretty considerate about it, even. He'd make a comment before going upstairs, or send a text to warn Chris away. And Chris didn't *mind* them starting in front of him, exactly, but…

But why hadn't he just walked away?

The answer was right there in front of him—*it was fucking hot*—but after twenty-six years of being disgusted when he was turned on, *why* was it fucking hot? Why hadn't he been appalled when they'd started? Why hadn't the sight of Gabriel squirming to get away from Aled's hands being a huge red flag and sent Chris fleeing into the next room? Why the hell had Chris' response been to—to—

He ran his hands over his bare scalp.

What the hell had happened?

Balance had been restored for the moment. He didn't want to touch his dick to clean it off. He didn't want to think about having sex. And the sounds had been stomach-turning—the wet slap of flesh, Gabriel gagging on cock, the squelching of his used—

Chris cleared his throat and stepped into the shower to ward off the memories and the urge to puke.

But at the same time, the disgust wasn't so strong as before.

And that was where Chris became unstuck. Sex had always disgusted him, ever since he'd found out what it was. It was the defining feature of his sexuality—sex was *gross*. It was the one thing that had plagued him since he was a child. He could accept being gay. He could maybe even accept being asexual, if there really were other men like him in that regard. But being so viscerally revolted by sex? That had been the thing that had kept him up at night. He could understand not being interested in sex, or not experiencing sexual attraction. But being outright *repulsed*? Chris couldn't get to grips with how that wasn't something awful.

Yet what had happened downstairs—at the time—hadn't been revolting.

It was *now*, in the clean shower cubicle with hot water washing away the evidence. But at the time, no.

And Chris didn't know what to do with that. Or how to figure out why it had been different.

Was it because —

Aled had been treating Gabriel like an object, and that was how Chris had always fucked him before. Like a thing. Like a better alternative to jacking off. Like a *doll*. When he screwed Gabriel in his sleep, it was like a warm sex toy. He wasn't going to move or talk or make demands or have an opinion. He wasn't going to judge. And when Gabriel climbed into his lap to ride him, it was like a business transaction. They talked about other things, both their minds pulled away from what was happening. No judging. No opinions. No *feeling*.

Deep down, way deep down where he was intensely ashamed of it, Chris knew that that was the point. He couldn't handle the possibility of being judged. He couldn't manage to let someone else see how appalled he was by the act itself, see how fucked up Chris really was underneath. So the way they'd always done it before was incredibly selfish. Get Chris' dick off, and to hell with what Gabriel wanted.

And downstairs had been —

The same, in a way.

But different.

Aled had been controlling the scenario. Talking to Gabriel, abusing him, calling him a whore and a slut and — and —

"Keeping him busy," Chris whispered.

Aled had kept him busy. As far as Gabriel was concerned, Chris hadn't been relevant. He was a dick. Aled was the one to watch out for, the one making threats, the one being dangerous. Chris had been background noise. Why pay any attention to Chris when it was Aled's hand around his throat and Aled's dick trying to strangle him from the inside out?

Chris swallowed dryly.

He had —

He'd enjoyed it.

The post-orgasmic satisfaction was unmistakeable. He'd not need to touch himself for a good couple of weeks after that. And he'd never fucked Gabriel *hard* like that. Never fucked anybody *hard*. His hips burned with the strain and it only added to the endorphin rush. His thighs ached from more than just this morning's run.

Chris felt *good*.

The shower stripped away the sweat and the smell, and by the time he stepped out, the raging confusion had settled into a gentler bewilderment. He still didn't really understand it, but he didn't feel quite so jarred either. It wasn't *that* different from what they'd already done, really. Gabriel had been so distracted by Aled choking him that he'd been effectively almost unaware of Chris, and certainly wouldn't have been thinking about it. And Chris just getting off in him like he was a *thing* had clearly been the point.

Hell, Chris knew Gabriel well enough to know that was the point of *most* of the games Gabriel played.

He'd just…never joined in before.

He dried himself off, smoothed some cream onto the eczema patch on his hip and headed into the master bedroom to get dressed. To his surprise, Aled was getting changed into his pyjamas.

"Where's Gabriel?"

"Locked him in the cupboard under the stairs," Aled said. "Going to play with him again later. You all right?"

"Bit confused," Chris admitted.

Aled paused, one leg in some ugly tartan pyjama bottoms.

"Want to talk about it?"

Ordinarily, Chris would have said no. But it wasn't like Aled hadn't gotten him to open up before, and...hell. They'd shared the same sex. Even if Chris had no intention of getting any closer to Aled's dick than the length of Gabriel's body, he couldn't exactly pretend they had to be proper and polite after *that*.

"I'm not even sure *how* to talk about it," Chris admitted, sitting on the edge of the bed to put his socks on. "I've never done anything like that before."

"Like a threesome, like the violence, like the humiliation...?"

Chris licked his lips. "All of it, really. But...I suppose the violence of it. That's what's throwing me. I've never — you know, I —"

He fumbled around for the words, yet Aled simply waited with the same calm patience as during their talk in the garden the first time.

"I've never wanted to join in with your sex games," Chris said eventually. "I've tried to avoid knowing any detail about them, to be honest. When we have sex, I'm trying my hardest to ignore that I'm actually having sex at all. But that — that felt different. Good. For me."

"Can I just...suggest something?"

"Okay."

"From what Gabriel's told me and the kind of things you said, you don't like it when you have to focus on the sex. If you can get it in and get off as fast as possible, then you will."

"Yeah."

"So it's not really any different to what just happened," Aled said. "You rammed it in him and you fucked him like a fleshlight. To hell with him. He was just a warm hole."

Chris blushed hotly.

"Hey, I'm not judging. Fucked him plenty like that myself. Definitely gets the job done. And he's never complained about it."

"He probably *should*..."

"Believe me, I've spent the last few years trying to figure why he likes being used and abused, but I've never found an answer," Aled chuckled. "Everyone likes what they like. He likes that. We don't really need to understand why at the end of the day."

"Guess not," Chris said, and blew out his cheeks. "I—my skin crawls and I feel so uncomfortable when I have sex because the act's pretty disgusting and *I* feel disgusting for doing it. And there's someone else right there, judging me in my birthday suit, judging what I'm doing. And the way me and Gabriel do it, it—it kind of...mitigates that."

"Mitigates it?"

"Yeah. We'll...have a conversation or something so he's not—you know, neither of us is paying attention to the sex. Or sometimes I'll do him while he's asleep so it's just over quickly for me and he can't—you know, he *can't* judge. He doesn't know until it's done. So he can't."

"Okay..."

"That was—kind of similar," Chris admitted. "He was too busy with you to think about me. I mean, you nearly choked him."

A smirk flickered across Aled's face, but he said nothing.

"So I could..." He grasped at his thoughts. "I've never fucked him that hard."

"You're missing a trick, then. He'll worship you for drilling him until it hurts."

Chris grimaced.

"Hey, it's true."

"I'll take your word for it," he said primly.

"Did you enjoy it, at least?"

Did he? When he stripped back the confusion and the anxiety?

"Yeah."

"Just surprised you did?"

"Yeah."

"Well, don't overthink it," Aled advised, shrugging on a T-shirt. "You know how the consent rules work, and you know he'll talk about it if he has second thoughts later. If you liked it and he liked it, then maybe try it again sometime."

"I feel like I need to figure out *why* I liked it, though."

"It helps," Aled admitted. "But sometimes it's just one of those things. I never found out why I like doing what I do. I've just had to accept it. And I can talk theories about Gabriel's tendencies, but it doesn't quite fit with the rest of his personality, so they don't quite work. But we work together. That's what matters. And if you both liked that, maybe try it another time. Maybe try tying him arse-up over the dining room table so he's available whenever you want. Maybe try making him wear a plug all day so all you have to do when the mood strikes is bend him over, rip it out, and shove yours in."

It sounded...scarily appealing.

"Don't get too caught up in why."

Chris nodded. He chewed over the questions one last time, then decided to lay them down. Maybe they could experiment a little with — with scenarios. Toys. Other stuff. But later down the line. Hell, he'd not even come to an understanding about his own sexuality, never mind whether kinky games were for him or not.

"Later I was going to tie him to the bed and do a bit of anal training with some toys," Aled said. "I can always leave him like that on the spare bed if you fancy trying out screwing him in bondage gear?"

"No thanks," Chris said. "I'm done for...a while now."

"God, you poor shit."

Chris snorted, the levity bursting the sombre mood like a popped bubble. "Are you kidding? I'd go insane if I needed it more often than once a fortnight."

"I'd go insane if I needed it *less* than once a day," Aled quipped, but grinned. "Come on. Let's make something good for dinner so he'll get hungry and offer sexual favours in return for getting to eat. He can get pretty inventive when he's desperate."

"You feed him anyway, right?"

"Depends on the favour."

Chris didn't — for once — ask any more questions.

Chapter Twenty-Four

Exactly five months after his accident, Gabriel walked back into the gym.

Wakefield had several gyms, but this one fancied itself the cream of the crop. It used to be a short walk from their old house, but was now a long bike ride, a bus and a long walk or a drop-off from Aled on his way to work. Not fancying the long walk, Gabriel got dropped off and kissed at the door before the gleaming car roared away towards Leeds and he was left to dip his toe back into real life.

And God, it felt good.

Gabriel didn't *use* the gym. Never had. His exercise was all sex and cycling, and it kept his body trim and his heart active. What did he need a sweaty old gym for?

No, he worked there. He'd started out mopping floors and changing toilet rolls and had worked his way up to customer services — giving tours, flirting people into memberships and answering the phone in the nicest voice he could muster. The work was menial, but his colleagues were fun and the customers almost fascinating. The gym ran the full range, from musclebound steroid abusers posing in front of the mirrors to little old ladies turning up every week for their pilates and yoga classes with more solemnity than churchgoers. He had friends there. Had met the occasional hookup through working there. Had people who knew him as he was now, with none of his ugly history to cloud their opinions. Gabriel had loved it.

Until he'd been hit by a bus.

He didn't have a right to sick pay. Jordan, his boss, had said he'd do his best to keep Gabriel's job open for him, but he couldn't make any promises after the first month. Gabriel had never had a guarantee he'd be able to come back.

Then something had finally gone his way, and Jordan had said yes.

"We've got the room," he'd said when Gabriel had called last month. "We picked up a load more customers in the summer. If you can get back before the Christmas lull, then I can get you back on the payroll."

And so here he was.

Walking back through the doors with his name badge on felt like closing a very dark and ugly chapter in his life.

"Gabriel!"

"How you doing, man?"

"Look who the cat dragged in…"

He'd been away an age, and many of the staff were students who came and went fairly quickly. Unfamiliar faces were everywhere. He didn't recognise the name of the duty manager on the rota. Someone who had been promoted from changing the layout of the weights section again, no doubt. But Sophie on the desk gave him the usual good-morning hug. The grumpy cleaner who worked the poolside called him a shyster and Gabriel laughed it off like always. Some of the Monday morning regulars — mostly pensioners who came to give their heart a little pep talk and watch daytime TV — said hello like he'd never been away.

He was on reduced hours and restricted duties, of course — no poolside tours for him, not until he stopped swaying altogether — but sinking into one of the desk chairs and calling IT to get his system passwords reset was euphoric. He could get some structure to his day. He could measure time by his own activities instead of when Aled was at work or whether Chris was out on a run. He'd get paid at the end of the month, even if it was a pittance. He could start contributing to the household bills again.

God, it felt good to be able to work.

Gabriel had been working since he was fourteen. Never great jobs — holding signs, knocking on doors, stacking shelves — but they were jobs all the same. Even when he'd been homeless, he'd had a job leafleting for a local takeaway. Even when he'd had nothing at all, he'd tried to pay his way. He hadn't always succeeded, but he'd tried. There'd always been *something*. It had got him through the worst periods in his life, the days when he'd wanted to lie down and never get back up again. Going to work had forced him to get up. Being without a job had felt *wrong*.

And the gym was the best job he'd ever had, so it felt like coming home. He flirted with Ben to make him blush. He spent his lunch hour talking to Gerald, a pensioner who'd been coming in daily since his wife died just to have something to do. He cooed over the photos of Gerald's new baby granddaughter all the way out in Australia. He entertained a couple of little kids while Katie signed their parents up to a family membership. He kept an eye on the door, wondering if Aled would pay a visit after work. Not that it would be anything more than a brief nod and polite smile, as if they didn't know each other. Gabriel liked this job so much that he'd never so much as kissed anyone on the premises, never mind had sex — and he'd not gone a single week at his previous place without shagging someone in the stockroom. But he wasn't going to risk this one. Not even for Aled and his filthy smirk.

But today, it seemed, Aled was going to let him readjust in peace.

It flew by. The hours rolled past like they hadn't since he'd stopped taking the good stuff in hospital, and before he knew it, it was time to go. His regulars shuffled out. Someone else's regulars shuffled in. The post-office rush hour filled up the carpark. Mumsy Fords with butterfly stickers and baby seats gave way to company Audis and gleaming BMWs from the business parks. At the end of his shift, he clocked off, got a goodbye hug from Sophie and walked out of the door.

And tomorrow he would come back and do it all again.

He didn't have a new bike yet, and in any case he didn't feel up to cycling again, but he'd expected Aled's car. Instead, Chris was lounging against the wall of the bike shed, waiting. He offered a hug. Gabriel stole a kiss, throwing caution to the wind. They walked up to the main road to wait for the bus, and Chris bitched about someone's dog on his morning run. They sat on the top deck, watching ominous clouds on the horizon, and paused in town for a coffee in the warm shelter of a Costa while the heavens opened. When it cleared, they made for their second bus and watched the town bleed away as they headed for Newmillerdam. Gabriel got a little motion sickness brewing in his throat and stomach, but nothing happened. Chris waited without a word at the bus stop round the corner from their house for Gabriel's nausea to settle. They walked back in step, and Chris started dinner while Gabriel put the laundry out on the line. By the time the risotto was ready to serve, Aled's car was grumbling to a halt on the driveway. Gabriel kissed him at the door and pushed him into a seat before climbing into his lap for a longer, deeper, hungrier sort of hello.

"Good day?" Aled asked with a grin.

Good?

Gabriel beamed. No, it had been better than good. It had been the best day since before he'd known what a bus could do to the human body.

"Yep."

"Work go well?"

"Yep."

"Good."

Gabriel laughed, squirming as his neck was bitten and arousal flickered into life.

"Oi. Food," Chris said.

"Yes, ma'am."

"Shurrup."

Gabriel was shooed to his seat, but he didn't care. Chris had warmed some crusty rolls, and called Gabriel disgusting for making a risotto sandwich. He didn't care about that, either. Aled held court for a while about whatever moron had designed the A61, they skirted carefully around some political story that Gabriel had missed but Chris and Aled clearly had opposing views

215

on, and—God, this was *life*. After so long in hospital and struggling to do silly, simple things like walk down the stairs or take a shower, Gabriel couldn't keep the grin off his face. He was back at work. The evening sun was burning their kitchen a deep rosy pink. Home-cooked food. Chris' feet between his own on the tiles, but Aled's bite stinging in his neck. He was going to have sex later. He could feel it in the air.

He had his life back.

Despite Aled's teeth-delivered promise, Gabriel was in no rush. They lingered over dessert—even Chris dug into a bowl of ice cream for once—then migrated as one to the living room and a horror movie that, surprisingly, had Aled on edge and Chris snickering at the dated effects. Gabriel just sat in the middle, Chris' hand locked between his thighs and Aled's arm around his waist, a thumb dangerously hooked into the waistband of his briefs.

"I'm going for a shower," Gabriel said when the credits rolled, and Aled gave him another bite.

"Come back down here after."

"In which case, I'm going to bed," Chris said.

Goodnight kisses were exchanged at the top of the stairs. Gabriel showered alone and marvelled at being able to do so. The only shadow of his long illness was the non-slip mat in the bottom of the cubicle and the wide-open door for someone to rescue him at a moment's notice.

Tipping his head back under the spray, Gabriel smiled.

He was *better*.

Maybe he'd never be absolutely right again. Cycling would have to wait and see. The motion sickness was persistent. He still swayed like a drunk at the tops of stairs or the edge of pavements, but he hadn't fallen or even stumbled in weeks. While the crippling migraines had healed along with the original bleed and the skull fracture, he'd been left with frequent dull headaches that beat against the same spot. Maybe they would never really go away.

But he could shower without clinging to another person. He could roll over in bed without freaking out. He could get the bus without being sick. He was back at work, the structure restored to his days and the money trickling back into his bank account.

He had his *life* back.

He could live with the motion sickness.

Because everything else was finally going right.

He went back downstairs naked. He had sex on the living room rug. He went to bed with bite marks all over his inner thighs.

And in the morning, when the sun rose, he got up to go to work, and started his life all over again.

Chapter Twenty-Five

It was raining, but Kevin's front door opened as Aled pulled up outside.

"Have fun," he said as Gabriel eased himself out of the back. "Ring if you need picking up today."

"Will do!"

He waited while Chris relocated to the front passenger seat, then waved to Kevin and pulled back out.

"Lunch?"

"Sure," Chris said, then surprised him. "Call it our third date."

"Our third date?"

"Yeah. Where you figure out if this is carrying on or we're calling it a day."

Aled raised his eyebrows, but didn't answer. He knew that something would need discussing now Gabriel was back at work and had no more need for a live-in nurse, but he hadn't expected Chris to come to *him* about it. He'd expected Gabriel to make the call, and for Aled to just hear about it all afterwards.

They didn't speak further as Aled headed back towards Wakefield, pulling off the A650 to a nice pub he knew. Chris could hang his diet for an hour. Pies were God's gift to food, and Aled wasn't going to be having a serious, potentially life-altering discussion over something inedible and flavourless like salad or hummus.

"Pie and a pint?" he asked as he pulled up into the little car park, and Chris grimaced.

"If I must."

"Yeah. You must."

"Fine."

The conversation was paused until they had at least their drinks and a secluded spot in one corner of the pub. It was reasonably busy—some kind of quiz gearing up on the other side of the building—so there was enough background noise to mask what they were talking about, but not so much they'd need to shout.

Perfect.

So Aled took full advantage and said, "You and I both know Gabriel wants you to stay."

Chris paused, lager halfway to his mouth. Then he set it down and nodded.

"So are you?"

Aled didn't like beating around the bush. Chris, however, seemed to specialise in going around entire forests before getting to the point.

"I've been asking myself the same question."

Case in point.

"You ask yourself a lot," Aled said. "Do you ever just answer?"

"Sometimes."

"Like when?"

"Like asking Gabriel out in the first place," Chris said.

Aled would give him that.

"But this is more complicated," Chris continued, and motioned between them. "This — we're not — you know."

"No," Aled agreed. "But I like you. We get on. We can make good friends, given the time and less stress."

And Aled tried to stay out of Gabriel's other relationships, but Chris' presence over the past couple of months...

It didn't quite feel like this was just Gabriel's relationship anymore. Aled wanted to know Chris' decision for himself, too. He wanted to know if he'd have a new friend in the area, or another person down south to visit now and then.

"I'm not interested, sexually or romantically," he said, and grinned as a little tension leaked out of Chris' shoulders. "You're not my type, and I can't see that changing. But I like you. I consider you a friend after all of this. And I'm not entirely asking about what your plans are just for Gabriel's sake."

Chris nodded, then bent his head to his lager. Aled gave him a minute to compose an answer. If he thought he dithered about taking chances sometimes, then Chris was a maestro.

"Here's the thing," Chris said eventually. "I like — being with you. Both of you. You're a nice guy and...well, obviously I like Gabriel. Not having to — to make plans to see him, getting to see him all the time, it's —"

He nodded. Trailed off. Started up again after another long drag on the edge of the glass.

"I'll miss you both when I go."

Aled worked his jaw.

"When you go."

Chris waved at the pub, shaking his head.

"This isn't me."

He didn't elaborate. For the first time, Aled wasn't entirely sure he needed him to. He knew what home felt like. And he knew how out of place it was to find it gone.

"So what now?" he asked.

Chris shrugged.

"Do we go back?" Aled asked. "You go back to Bristol and snatching a visit every few months when you or he can get out of work?"

"I don't know."

"Neither of you want to. *I* don't want you to."

"I know," Chris said.

"So stay."

He'd never thought he'd ask. Hell, when Gabriel had moved in, Aled had wanted nothing less than one of his other men in the house. But somehow...

Now it would feel empty without Chris' bike in the corner, without the health food in the fridge, without the snick of the door closing behind him as he went for his morning runs. Three in the living room watching the TV instead of two. The thrill of snatched sex in the bathroom, pretending at an affair while the oblivious boyfriend puttered about in the next room. Being ganged up on, or getting to gang up on Gabriel.

Pies and pints.

Aled had missed simple company over pies and pints.

"I can't," Chris said, shaking his head. "I feel like a fish out of water up here. Being with the two of you is great, and I want to keep that. But it's like a foreign country to me. I never wanted to live up north, and this hasn't changed that. I'm itching to go home."

Aled chewed on the corner of his lip.

"How about *you* change, for once?"

Aled blinked, brought up short.

"Sorry?"

"I know your story," Chris said. "Gabriel moved into the bedroom you shared with your ex-wife. Gabriel dumped a guy for you—"

Aled's temper flared. "That was—"

"I know it was a good thing, but it was still for you in the beginning," Chris said. "He lives with you so he naturally does a lot of things because they fit with you. But—I'm down south. And so are your family. Your sister and her nephew."

Aled drew back, frowning.

"I want you and Gabriel nearby," Chris said. "But I'm a southerner. So is he, technically speaking. And so is your family. You're the only thing anchoring anyone to the north, mate."

Footsteps on worn carpet. Steaming pies on hot plates banged down between. Aled answered questions about condiments through numb lips, then narrowed his eyes into a frown as the waiter retreated once more.

"You think we should move south?" he asked.

Chris raised his glass. "Just think about it, yeah?"

Aled had never considered it before. Kevin was here. Their jobs were here. When Suze had married and left, Nan and Gabriel's granddad had been here.

But now—

"Maybe it's time to start again," Chris suggested.

Maybe—after nearly five years—it was time to go back to the beginning.

Want to see more from this author?
Here's a taster for you to enjoy!

Enough
Matthew J. Metzger

Excerpt

He could smell the fire.

He was blind. His eyes streamed. The curling wallpaper crackled and hissed. His skin was burning. The air in his lungs seared him from the inside out. And there was nowhere to go — no escape from the heat, no escape from the orange towers and acrid black smoke, no *air*.

"Ezra!"

The smoke wrapped itself around his teeth and tongue like a grotesque mockery of a kiss, and there was no reply but the roar of hot air and climbing fire. The house was burning. *The house was burning!*

"Ezra! Ez!"

A scream. A piercing scream, like nothing he'd ever heard, but before he could move, the wooden boards crumbled to ash and he was falling, tearing through the shreds of stairs into the inferno, and —

Jesse hit the carpet with a thump and jarred himself awake.

The flat was quiet. The streetlight touched the other side of the curtains with a faint orange light. There was no smoke, no fire, no sound. Nothing.

Jesse dragged himself back onto the bed. The sheets were impossibly tangled and his tank top stuck to him with sweat. His wrist ached in its brace where he'd bumped it, but the panic hadn't quite eased its grip on his heart or his lungs, and he fumbled for his phone, ignoring the pain.

Thank God for speed dial.

The clock on the side said two-fifty-eight, and the phone rang six times before the line coughed and crackled and a sleepy voice, tinged in the early hours with the fading edges of a Welsh accent, mumbled a vague sort of question.

"Ez?"

There was a rustle of sheets. "Jesse?"

"Oh, God," Jesse breathed. The air escaped in a rush, loud and hard. His lungs shook with the effort. "Shit. I just— I needed to check—"

"Jess? What's happened, sweetheart?"

The soft roll of his vowels, the accent entirely muted when he was properly awake, was as comforting as a hug, and Jesse coughed out, "Nightmare," before thinking twice. Ezra was okay. He was okay. It was all okay.

"Oh, sweetheart," Ezra murmured, low and crooning. "Do you want to tell me about it?"

"I need—can I come over? I know it's late and I know you have work in the morning, but—I just—I need—"

"No," Ezra interrupted, and Jesse's stomach twisted violently.

"*Please*, Ez, I—"

"Hey, hey, hey." Ezra cut him off. "Hey, stop, calm down, sweetheart. I *meant* you can't come here. You don't sound okay, not to me, and I don't want you to go out like this, so I'll come to you, all right?"

Jesse exhaled, the twist easing. "Okay."

"You okay if I hang up, or do you want me to put the phone on speaker?"

"Can—speaker," Jesse swallowed against the nausea. He was still shaking, he realised faintly. "I just—I couldn't find you, Ez. The house was burning and I couldn't find you, and I—I need to hear you. You don't have to talk to me, but I need to hear you."

"Okay." The phone crackled again and clunked, and suddenly Ezra's voice was loud and echoing. Soothing. The Welsh hint was fading, and Jesse could suddenly hear him dressing, but he was *there*. "Was it my house or the one last week?"

"Yours," Jesse said. "I was on the stairs, and they gave way, and I woke up. I couldn't find you."

"If my house was on fire, I would probably be in the kitchen having caused it," Ezra said, and yawned loudly. "Make yourself useful, sweetheart, and make up a brew for me? I've not slept long."

Jesse knew better than to apologise. He shrugged out of his sweat-soaked pyjamas and pulled on a pair of jogging bottoms before taking the phone through the narrow hall into the kitchen. The kitchen window overlooked the main road. A police car trailed idly by on the prowl. Phone to his ear, he listened to Ezra swear sleepily at his cupboard, and the soft sounds of those narrow feet padding downstairs.

"Sweetheart?"

"Mm?" Jesse listened to the front door and the heavy sound of the key.

"I'm going to hang up while I drive. You all right for ten minutes until I get there?"

"Yeah," Jesse croaked. His heart had come down out of the rafters, and he could breathe. The streetlights didn't look threatening anymore. He just felt...shaky. Sick and shaky and scared. "Yeah, Ez, I'll be fine."

"Okay. Love you."

The dial tone was immediate. Jesse dropped the phone to the counter and switched on the kettle, staring out of the window and waiting, arms folded against the chill. It wasn't the first nightmare, and it wouldn't be the last. He usually managed one a week without fail, and the injury hadn't helped matters. But they didn't usually involve Ezra in burning buildings. They didn't usually involve losing him.

And Jesse couldn't stomach the thought of losing him.

Which was a bit scary in itself. They'd only met eight months ago. At a gay bar, of all places — the one place where he went to meet sex partners, not partner partners. Jesse had thought the freckled blond with the dark eyes was pretty in the neon lights and had bought him a drink, talked him into a dance, bought him another. Kissed him at the back of the dance floor — and had promptly found himself alone, but with a phone number in his back pocket.

He'd wanted sex. That was all he'd been after. Sex with a pretty guy. But then they'd gone on a date and he'd met Ezra properly, and he was lost. Ezra wasn't just a handsome face and nice legs. Ezra was the world. He was Jesse's world, and it had only been eight months, but Jesse still knew that this was it, for him. Ezra was it. There would never be anyone else like him.

So he stood in a tense vigil at the window, waiting for the faithful little Peugeot 207 to creep around the corner. Waiting for Ezra to come, because there was emotional shock and there was sense, and the two weren't in line right now. He knew Ezra was okay. He knew it. He'd answered the phone. He'd been sleepy and understanding and sworn at his cupboard. He was fine.

But Jesse still needed to reach out and touch him, just to make sure. *Somehow.*

The little blue car was lonely on the three-in-the-morning road, and Jesse propped the door of his flat to creep down the communal stairs and open the main door. Ezra had gotten sort-of dressed, in jeans and an open check shirt, feet shoved into his trainers without socks, and his hair was wild and fluffy, in gleeful disarray, as he locked the car and wrapped himself around Jesse in a tight, warm hug.

Jesse clung back until something creaked, and pressed the side of his face against that wild hair.

"You're all right, sweetheart," Ezra murmured.

Jesse squeezed again until Ezra's grip on the nape of his neck tightened in warning, then he let go and dragged Ezra up the silent stairs by the hand. Concrete stairs. They wouldn't collapse in a fire until the whole building came down.

He didn't say a word until he'd pressed the requested tea into Ezra's hands, locked the door again and bundled them both back to the messy bed. Ezra was equally silent, taking a couple of mouthfuls before abandoning the tea, stripping to his underwear and crawling into the mess to mould himself into Jesse's arms.

"There you go," he murmured lowly, kissing Jesse's encroaching stubble and stroking a hand gently through his hair. "Feel better now?"

"Mm," Jesse pressed his nose into Ezra's neck, tangling their legs together. He could feel a strong pulse in Ezra's jugular. He could feel the rough skin of the bumpy scar on Ezra's shoulder under his fingertips. He could feel the fuzzy mess of Ezra's hair, usually styled and stiff in that messy-but-it's-on-purpose-so-it's-okay manner, now just loose and wild. He could feel *him*. "Thank you."

"Thank me again tomorrow afternoon when I'm grumpy and exhausted after two hours of the Year Nines."

"Okay," Jesse agreed, sliding his arms completely around Ezra's back until he enveloped him. They didn't often sleep cuddled together — or even together at all, between Ezra's eight-to-four and Jesse's shifts — but he needed this. He *needed* it.

"Mind if I go to sleep?"

"No," Jesse squirmed until Ezra got the hint and tucked his head under his chin. His hair tickled. Jesse kissed the top of his head and wished he had the easy grace with language that Ezra did. Wished he could express himself properly. Wished he could talk as easily as he hugged. But all that came out was, "I just needed to touch you."

Ezra said nothing to that, simply shifting until he was comfortable, one arm over Jesse's ribs and the other tucked over his own waist in a casual sort of drop. Ezra was *long* — long limbs, long neck, all willowy lines and bendy joints, and he settled like water into the bulkier, stiffer contours of Jesse's body.

But he fit, and he fit perfectly, and Jesse wrapped him up and held him, breathing in the smell of store-brand shampoo and cheap aftershave until the last traces of the nightmare-induced fear washed away.

It was still a long time before he slept.

Sign up for our newsletter and find out about all our romance book releases, eBook sales and promotions, sneak peeks and FREE romance books!

About the Author

Matthew J. Metzger is an asexual, transgender British author juggling books, an office job and a love of travel with the human need for sleep once in a while. He writes both adult and young adult books focusing on LGBT+ characters and their relationships, particularly those from the less salubrious areas in which he was dragged up over the years.

On the very rare occasions that Matt isn't writing, he can usually be found at the gym, halfway up a mountain or collecting new tattoos. (And yes, he does have book ink...)

Matthew loves to hear from readers. You can find his contact information, website details and author profile page at https://www.pride-publishing.com